LOVE BY THE LAKE

BARBARA CARTLAND

Barbara

.com

POD Preparation by M-Y Books
m-ybooks.co.uk

THE BARBARA CARTLAND PINK COLLECTION

Barbara Cartland was the most prolific bestselling author in the history of the world. She was frequently in the Guinness Book of Records for writing more books in a year than any other living author. In fact her most amazing literary feat was when her publishers asked for more Barbara Cartland romances, she doubled her output from 10 books a year to over 20 books a year, when she was 77.

She went on writing continuously at this rate for 20 years and wrote her last book at the age of 97, thus completing 400 books between the ages of 77 and 97.

Her publishers finally could not keep up with this phenomenal output, so at her death she left 160 unpublished manuscripts, something again that no other author has ever achieved.

Now the exciting news is that these 160 original unpublished Barbara Cartland books are ready for publication and they will be published by Barbaracartland.com exclusively on the internet, as the web is the best possible way to reach so many Barbara Cartland readers around the world.

The 160 books will be published monthly and will be numbered in sequence.

The series is called the Pink Collection as a tribute to Barbara Cartland whose favourite colour was pink and it became very much her trademark over the years.

The Barbara Cartland Pink Collection is published only on the internet. Log on to www.barbaracartland.com to find out how you can purchase the books monthly as they are published, and take out a subscription that will ensure that all subsequent editions are delivered to you by mail order to your home.

TITLES IN THIS SERIES

THE LATE DAME BARBARA CARTLAND

Barbara Cartland, who sadly died in May 2000 at the grand age of ninety eight, remains one of the world's most famous romantic novelists. With worldwide sales of over one billion, her outstanding 723 books have been translated into thirty six different languages, to be enjoyed by readers of romance globally.

Writing her first book "Jigsaw" at the age of 21, Barbara became an immediate bestseller. Building upon this initial success, she wrote continuously throughout her life, producing bestsellers for an astonishing 76 years. In addition to Barbara Cartland's legion of fans in the UK and across Europe, her books have always been immensely popular in the USA. In 1976 she achieved the unprecedented feat of having books at numbers 1 & 2 in the prestigious B. Dalton Bookseller bestsellers list.

Although she is often referred to as the "Queen of Romance", Barbara Cartland also wrote several historical biographies, six autobiographies and numerous theatrical plays as well as books on life, love, health and cookery. Becoming one of Britain's most popular media personalities and dressed in her trademark pink, Barbara spoke on radio and television about social and political issues, as well as making many public appearances.

In 1991 she became a Dame of the Order of the British Empire for her contribution to literature and her work for humanitarian and charitable causes.

Known for her glamour, style, and vitality Barbara Cartland became a legend in her own lifetime. Best remembered for her wonderful romantic novels and loved by millions of readers worldwide, her books remain treasured for their heroic heroes, plucky heroines and traditional values. But above all, it was Barbara Cartland's overriding belief in the positive power of love to help, heal and improve the quality of life for everyone that made her truly unique.

"True love is a sacred flame
That burns eternally,
And none can dim its special glow
Or change its destiny.
True love speaks in tender tones
And hears with gentle ear.
True love gives with open heart
And true love conquers fear.
True love makes no harsh demands
It neither rules nor binds,
And true love holds with gentle hands
The hearts that it entwines."

"This is an ancient traditional poem of love and has
always been one of my favourites."

Barbara Cartland

CHAPTER ONE
1873

"The Master wants to see you, my Lady," the maid called, putting her head round the door.

Lolita looked up and sighed.

She knew this meant a row.

Her stepfather had come into the room at the moment when Murdock Tanner was trying to kiss her. She was struggling violently against him and as her stepfather entered she had struck him in the face.

She had managed to escape and ran out of the room upstairs to her bedroom.

She was fully aware that now there would be an explosion.

Murdock Tanner was enormously rich and of great importance to her stepfather, Ralph Piran, an exceedingly successful shipping magnate. He had made a huge fortune from the steamers now sailing daily across the Atlantic to New York and to other parts of the world.

Yet because he was greedy he wanted still more. He had found it very convenient to marry Lolita's mother after her father the Earl of Walcott and Vernon had died unexpectedly.

The Earl had been in an accident late at night when the drivers of two chaises had dined over well and were travelling too fast and the one driven by the Earl had overturned.

One of the horses rolled on him and if he had survived he would have undoubtedly been a cripple for life, which was something he would have loathed.

Lolita could only think it was in a way a blessing that he had died without realising what had happened to him.

He had however left her and her mother penniless.

The Earl had been a gambler all his life and because he was very much in love with her mother, she had in many ways been a good influence over him, but she could not prevent him taking a chance on a card, a horse race or anything else which offered a sporting gamble.

After the funeral the Countess had sat down with her daughter Lolita and they had tried to work out what they could do.

The answer of course was nothing.

During the years she had been married, the Countess had gradually lost touch with her family as they lived in the North of England and her husband claimed hardly any family relations.

The Earldoms of Walcott and Vernon had been united three hundred years ago, but the present Earl had dropped the double name because he found it so cumbersome. He arranged that the family would use the name of Vernon while he was the Earl of Walcott only.

Apart from the ancient name and a history which spoke of noble deeds and distinguished statesmen, the Earl boasted no possessions and a very small income.

It just enabled him and his wife to live in a house in an undistinguished street in London. Because they saved and he was occasionally successful at the card tables, they managed to take a holiday abroad every year.

Unfortunately the Earl enjoyed going to Baden-Baden and Monte Carlo and visiting their casinos. Inevitably they returned home poorer than when they had started.

There were, however, times when he won and then because he loved his wife and his daughter he insisted on buying them expensive presents, which later had to be sold.

At the same time they loved him, because apart from everything else he was a great gentleman.

But that was something Lolita could not say about her stepfather.

It had, however, been impossible for her mother to refuse Ralph Piran. He was quite presentable although not of the same class as the Earl.

His father had been Captain of a ship and this meant he was engrossed with the sea from the moment he was born. His mother had been the daughter of a Solicitor, who had taught his grandson everything he himself knew about money and as soon as Ralph could think he was determined to be rich.

He had a very shrewd brain and by the time he was twenty-five he had accumulated an income which was the envy of his contemporaries.

He soon decided that his friends and acquaintances were not good enough for him.

He wanted to shine in the Social world as well as among those who admired his business prowess and when by chance he met the Countess of Walcott, she was the answer to many of the ambitions that had driven him since he had left school.

The Countess was extremely unhappy after her husband's death, but that did not deter Ralph Piran. If riches could make her happy that was what he was prepared to give her.

He also wanted a son who would carry on his ever-expanding business, but here, however, he was disappointed.

But it gave him some satisfaction that Lolita at seventeen was outstandingly beautiful and he could say to those he met in the business world,

"I must introduce you to my stepdaughter, Lady Lolita Vernon."

This year Lolita was eighteen and he was determined that the Social world should help him celebrate the occasion.

He had already bought a large and impressive house in Berkeley Square and he was planning a 'coming out' ball for Lolita. He was determined it would be more sensational than any other ball given throughout the Season.

Then at the end of April, when her mother was making all the necessary arrangements for Lolita to be presented at Court, she suffered a stroke.

Not even the doctors could explain why it had happened. The stroke sent her into a coma from which the most skilled and the most expensive of the medical practitioners could not rouse her.

This of course upset the plans for Lolita as a *debutante*, as it was quite impossible for her to stage a ball in the same house where her mother lay unconscious.

It also meant that Ralph Piran had to find hostesses amongst his wife's friends who would chaperone Lolita when she appeared in public.

He was determined that she should continue with her Season as it helped him not only socially but in his business.

It was still considered vulgar by the Social hostesses for a gentleman to be in trade and Ralph Piran was determined to be accepted.

He was rich enough, he believed, to buy himself a position in the Social world which he was so determined to achieve.

Apart from his money his greatest asset was his stepdaughter.

He himself was actually quite presentable, being tall, dark-haired and good-looking. Dressed by the most expensive tailors in London he was able to mingle with members of White's Club and Boodles without anyone questioning why he was amongst them.

It was however a different problem when it came to invitations. A large number of Social hostesses had been very fond of the Countess of Walcott.

Distressed by her illness, they had invited Lolita to luncheon and dinner and a ball when they gave one, but they did not invite her stepfather.

It made him angry, but he kept his feelings to himself and he made sure, when it was at all possible, that he was at parties where among the other guests were the hostesses who had barred their doors to him.

Lolita was well aware of the presents which passed from her stepfather to the mothers of her friends and she knew they could not afford to offer such generous hospitality unless, to put it bluntly, it was subsidised.

Ralph Piran was exceedingly jealous and by the end of May he had attended a number of balls to which he would not have received an invitation earlier in the year.

He got what he wanted cleverly and tactfully.

Men clapped him on the back and told him he was 'a good fellow'. At the same time they borrowed a thousand pounds from him and he gave it to them willingly.

He was not so foolish, however, as to neglect his business because of his social ambitions.

He was in the middle of pulling off a deal that would make him the owner of a whole fishing fleet which he had always wanted to buy.

It was, however, such an expensive purchase that he was obliged to accept help from some of his friends, who were as interested as he was in multiplying their money and increasing the number of ships they possessed.

Murdock Tanner had for some years been the most important and most successful entrepreneur in the shipping industry. If he and these friends of his became partners, Piran knew they would take control of the seas and oceans which covered nearly three-quarters of the world.

Murdock Tanner was growing old and like Ralph Piran he had no son. He had already hinted when they were negotiating with each other that Ralph would be his heir.

Ralph Piran entered the hall of his house in Berkeley Square and strode towards his study.

As he did so he heard Lolita scream.

He could not imagine what the matter was until he opened the door and saw her fighting savagely with Murdock Tanner.

Even as he stood transfixed in the doorway, she slapped Murdock on the face.

As he recoiled from the blow, she managed to twist herself from his arms and ran past him through the door.

He could hear her footsteps gather speed as she crossed the hall and tore up the stairs.

Ralph Piran hurried forward with apologies and hastily provided his guest with a glass of champagne.

Lolita reached her bedroom, slammed the door behind her and sank down at her dressing table. She looked in the mirror at her dishevelled hair.

'How dare he try to kiss me?' she fumed. 'If Mama had been here she would have been furious.'

Before she fell ill, Lolita's mother had told her over and over again how to behave correctly as a *debutante*.

"You must be quiet, modest and polite, darling," she had said, "and of course never do anything that would get you talked about."

"What do you mean, Mama?" Lolita had asked her.

Her mother hesitated for a moment before she replied,

"Some girls, I am told, allow men to become too familiar with them. You must of course never go into the garden or into an empty room alone with a man."

"You mean, Mama, that he would try to kiss me?"

"It is something a gentleman should not do," her mother answered. "At the same time I am told girls encourage men in a way that in my day would have been considered very fast and badly behaved."

She smiled before she went on,

"I want you to marry someone charming and of course as well bred as your father."

Lolita was intelligent enough to realise that her mother was warning her and it was against the sort of men who Ralph Piran was bound to associate with in his business.

She had met some of them because her stepfather always wanted to show her off.

She had thought them rather coarse and what her mother would have considered too familiar.

The older men chucked her under the chin and told her she was pretty enough to break the hearts of all the men in town.

The young men held her hand too tightly and she was sure if she had danced with them they would hold her too close.

This, in fact, did not happen because they were not invited to the balls given by her mother's friends and neither were those who accepted a little help secretly from her stepfather.

She enjoyed all the balls she attended and yet she thought they would be far more interesting if her mother had still been with her.

Lolita was aware that because her stepfather was so rich, the Dowagers sitting round the walls whispered whenever she appeared.

Quite a number of gentlemen who would otherwise have ignored her and preferred to dance with older women partnered her in waltzes.

She had enough brains to realise what was going on when a young man had been told how rich her stepfather was. He paid her fulsome compliments and made pointed suggestions that he should be invited to their house in Berkeley Square.

Now that her mother was so ill, Lolita found herself acting as hostess to her stepfather's friends.

She thought in the past they would have met him in the City, but for the last three days Murdock Tanner, who had, Lolita learned, come to London on business, had been continually with them at the house.

The first time she had seen him she thought him uncouth and unpleasant, but she had been polite to him because she knew he was important to her stepfather.

He told her she was 'a very pretty piece' and that her eyes were like diamonds. He had even indicated that he would like to give her some.

Lolita had been polite, but she considered he had a somewhat debauched expression on his face and was repulsed by the way he ate and some of the remarks he made.

While her stepfather could just about get by in the smartest Society, there was no chance where Murdock Tanner was concerned.

He was rough and vulgar and Lolita was quite certain from the way he ate he had never been taught any table manners.

However, her stepfather talked to him with respect and admiration and Lolita did not have to be told how exceedingly rich Murdock Tanner was.

She avoided him whenever possible, but last night, when she learned that once again he was dining in the house, it had been a relief to know that she was going out to a small party given by one of her mother's friends.

Lolita had enjoyed herself.

She had, however, come home early and was halfway up the stairs, when she heard Murdock Tanner emerge from the study with her stepfather. He was talking loudly in his thick, rather coarse voice.

Lolita hurried up the last flight of stairs and as she reached the landing she heard him stumble. She realised that he had drunk too much when he swore several unpleasant oaths.

'He is a ghastly man,' she told herself, going quickly into her bedroom and locking the door.

She had not gone down to breakfast the following morning until she learned that her stepfather had left. She was glad that she was going out to luncheon with some friends just in case he returned with Murdock Tanner.

When she came home she thought that there was no one downstairs, so she walked to her stepfather's study to find the newspapers, which were always put on a stool in front of the fireplace.

When she opened the door it was to find to her consternation that Murdock Tanner was standing looking out of the window.

He turned round as she entered and came towards her.

He asked her where she had been hiding as he had not seen her last night.

"I went to a party," Lolita answered, "but not a very large one and I enjoyed myself very much."

"Of course you did," Murdock Tanner said, "looking as pretty as a picture and turning all the young men's heads. How many of them kissed you?"

Lolita thought it was an insulting remark and replied,

"No one! I do not allow men to kiss me."

"Then you're missing something very pleasant and I'll show you, pretty little creature, how it should be done."

To her astonishment he put out his arms and drew her against him.

For a moment she could hardly believe it was happening.

As she struggled she realised he was very strong and as his arms tightened she realised he was going to kiss her.

It was then that she began to fight against him with all the strength she could find.

She sensed that he was amused by her resistance, but was determined to have his own way.

"No! No!" she exclaimed as his lips touched her cheek.

With a frantic effort she managed to free one arm and struck him in the face.

It was as he recoiled from the blow that Murdock Tanner realised that someone had entered the room.

As his grip loosened Lolita managed to free herself.

It was all so unpleasant that having reached her bedroom she washed her face and her hands. She felt she was washing away the disgust the man had aroused in her.

She told herself that she had no intention of going downstairs again until he had left.

Now that her stepfather had sent for her, she could only hope that he had gone.

To make sure, she questioned the maid,

"Is my stepfather alone?"

"Yes, my Lady, his visitor left a little while ago."

Lolita felt she could hardly refuse to go to her stepfather now that he had sent for her, but equally she was quite certain it would be an unpleasant interview.

She tidied her hair and brushed down her dress as if she was brushing away Murdock Tanner because he had touched it.

Then she walked very slowly downstairs and towards her stepfather's study.

He was sitting at his writing desk when she came in through the door and she knew at once that he was in one of his rages.

Those who worked for him and his servants dreaded the moment when the boss was 'put out'.

He would start by being icily cold and then his voice, which was like a whiplash, would grow sharper and louder until finally he was shouting at whoever had upset him.

Lolita had often thought that strong men would turn pale when he raged at them and she could only be thankful that he had never, since he had been married, let her mother see him in a towering rage.

She thought it was not only love but respect which had made him gentle with her Mama, but he did not extend this courtesy to her.

Lolita had experienced several heated arguments and on one occasion he had almost lost his temper, but now when she looked at him she felt as if a cold hand was squeezing her heart as she realised how very angry he was.

She moved towards the fireplace and he rose from behind the writing desk to join her.

"What the devil do you mean by being so offensive to my friend Murdock Tanner?" he demanded.

"He was being offensive to me."

"By trying to kiss you?" her stepfather asked. "Good God, girl! What harm can that do? You should be honoured that a man as clever and successful as Tanner should admire you as he does – "

"I don't want his admiration," said Lolita firmly. "He is old, ugly and unpleasant – he has no right to touch me."

Ralph Piran laughed and it was an unpleasant sound.

"So you are giving yourself airs and graces," he snarled, "and who is paying for them? *I am*. How do you think your mother could have afforded the gown you have on now? Or the dozens of others you have upstairs in your wardrobe?"

His voice grew louder as he continued,

"I am paying for you, and Murdock Tanner, as he is my partner, has contributed too. Do you understand we are partners? I will not have him insulted by a stupid little fool like you."

Now he was shouting and Lolita thought that his eyes were flashing at her almost as if he had lights behind them.

"I will – not – allow," she managed to stammer, "Murdock Tanner or – any other man to – kiss me unless – I love him. That is what Mama would – expect."

"As she cannot tell you so," Ralph Piran snapped, "you will listen to me and obey me. If Murdock Tanner wants to kiss you, you are not to refuse him, but kiss him back."

"Whatever you may say, Step-papa, I will not let him – come near me!" she retorted. "*He is repulsive*! It makes me sick even to let him touch my hand!"

"So you are defying me, Miss Hoity-Toity!" he howled. "Let me tell you one thing and you had better get it into your thick head – if Murdock Tanner wants to kiss you and you refuse him, I will beat you until you allow him to do so!"

Lolita gave an audible gasp, but he went on,

"There is just a chance that he might want to marry you. If so, I will give the marriage my blessing and if you refuse him, I will drag you to the altar, even if you are as senseless as your mother is at the moment."

At the word marriage Lolita had stiffened and stood still as if turned to stone.

She could hardly believe it possible. Yet her stepfather would not have spoken about marriage if it had not been in his mind.

The whole idea was so frightening and so horrifying that she just stared at him.

"Those are my orders and if you do not obey me, you will find it very painful until you do."

He moved forward as if he was either about to strike Lolita or shake her.

Her scream echoed round the study as she ran across the room and pulled the door open.

Although she heard him shout after her, she did not hear what he said as she rushed upstairs to her bedroom.

She locked the door behind her and flung herself down on the bed shaking all over from shock.

After some minutes she realised that there was nothing she could do about what had happened.

She remembered now that, since Murdock Tanner had been coming to the house so frequently, she had thought that he looked at her in an unpleasant way.

She could not explain it to herself, but now she guessed he had been appraising her, as if she was a cargo he had been deciding whether or not to buy.

She realised that if he wanted her, it would further her stepfather's business and his fortune and he would therefore do everything in his power, as he had just warned her, to make her accept Murdock Tanner.

'It's incredible, impossible, and I will not do it,' Lolita murmured.

At the same time she had no idea how she could protect herself.

She was sure her stepfather was not exaggerating when he threatened to beat her if she did not comply with what he wanted.

There were stories of him when in a rage beating the young boys on one of his ships and it was whispered that one of the boys in the office had to be treated by a doctor. Lolita had not paid much attention to such tales at the time.

She was not particularly interested in her stepfather's business and she did not want to become involved with anything that was not her concern.

It had been easy when her mother had been there and they had talked together about everything except her stepfather's business.

When her mother talked about her father, there was always a softness in her eyes.

Her voice told Lolita quite clearly that she still loved him.

'It was for my sake,' she thought now, 'that Mama married Ralph Piran. She could not bear that I should be so poor that I could not afford a gown to go to the ball. She wanted me to meet the sort of people she had known when she was a girl.'

She wished she could go and tell her mother what had just happened, but she just lay still with closed eyes. The nurses looking after her were not very hopeful that she would ever regain her senses.

'I cannot speak to Mama,' Lolita said to herself, 'and there is no one else who would understand how horrifying and ghastly my situation has become.'

Then almost as if it was an answer to a prayer, she knew that *she must run away*.

If she stayed, however much she might resist her stepfather, he would eventually force her to do what he wanted.

If Murdock Tanner wanted to marry her, he would, as he had said, drag her unconscious to the altar.

'What can I do?' she asked again, but the answer was already in her mind.

It was then that she dragged herself off her bed and sat down to think her situation out carefully and clearly.

She needed to be quite certain that she did not make any mistakes, as if she did run away and was caught, her stepfather would be so angry he would lock her in her room and it would be impossible for her to escape a second time.

'If I leave,' she said to herself, 'I have will have to leave for good. But where can I hide?'

As she had often recognised, no one had fewer relations than she. The cousins her mother had sometimes spoken about lived far away in a part of England she had never visited.

She mulled over the friends she had made since she turned eighteen and a *debutante* and she was quite certain none of them would take her part against her stepfather.

There was no young man to whom she could turn for protection. They had danced with her, flattered her and even sent flowers to Berkeley Square and she always had the uneasy feeling that they were thinking how much money she would have rather than about herself.

If she would ask any of them to elope with her, she suspected they would refuse to do so.

Actually she had no desire to elope with anyone nor to marry any of the men who paid her compliments.

16

She did not know what she was waiting for, but she vaguely thought of it as love.

Something very beautiful and very wonderful and when she found it she would be as happy as her mother had been with her father.

Whatever the difficulties, however hard-up they were, they had always seemed blissfully content with each other.

Lolita knew that when her father died, part of her mother died with him.

'How could I ever feel like that for a man like Murdock Tanner?' she asked herself. Then she shuddered because the very idea was revolting.

Now the pride which she had always been told ran in her blood came to her assistance. It told her that unless she was to surrender completely to her stepfather' demands, she must go away.

She had her health and her strength.

She must make a life for herself away from him and the horror and menace of Murdock Tanner.

'I will leave tomorrow morning,' Lolita decided, 'but I shall have to be very clever because otherwise Step-papa will find me and force me back.'

She remembered that they were dining out together tonight and that the dinner was being given by a rather dubious Society hostess in Belgravia.

She was someone that Lolita suspected her stepfather had 'helped' to host a ball to which he would be invited. It had been a success, but the guests were not as smart or influential as those at other parties Lolita had attended.

Tonight it was to be a party of twenty or thirty guests and everyone would dance after dinner and she would have to dance with her stepfather.

'He will have recovered his temper by that time,' Lolita calculated. 'I will be nice to him, so that he will think I am agreeing to everything he has suggested.'

She stood up from the stool and walked next door into the wardrobe room, which not only contained her clothes but some of her luggage. She found one case which was lighter than the rest.

Lolita thought if the worst came to the worst, she could carry it if she did not pack too much.

She made sure that all the doors were locked so that no one could surprise her by coming in unexpectedly and then she packed the things she thought she would need immediately.

Besides her underclothes she included three day-dresses and three simple evening-gowns, all made of very light material, but there was not much room left in the case for anything else.

Then she put it away in the cupboard and hid the key as it was important that none of the maids should find it and think it strange.

She next had to think out and plan how she could find some ready money – this was not at all easy.

She only needed to order anything she wanted from a shop and the account would be sent to her stepfather and all bills were paid by his accountant.

Lolita had a little pocket money of course for her contributions in Church or if she had to tip anyone in a cloakroom or a man who fetched her carriage for her.

When she counted out what she had in her handbag it came to only a few pounds.

'I shall need a lot more than that,' she concluded.

She sat down again to think it all over very carefully – just the way her father did when he lost all his money gambling and needed some more to have another chance.

She remembered that her mother possessed a large amount of very valuable jewellery which Ralph Piran had given her.

She did not want to touch the jewellery, which she knew was in the safe, but there might be some money stored with it.

The safe was situated in a small room between her mother's and her stepfather's bedrooms so that either of them could use it at any time they wished. Lolita knew where the key was kept and had opened it many times for her mother.

She went to the door of her bedroom and listened. She wanted to know if there was anyone about and if her stepfather was still in the study.

If he was, it was unlikely he would come upstairs to the safe and if he had gone out, it would be better still.

The house seemed very quiet and there was only the sound of carriages driving round Berkeley Square.

Lolita slipped along the passage, passing the room where her mother lay in a coma. She quietly opened the door and tiptoed up to the safe.

It was, the manufacturer had assured Ralph Piran, the most up-to-date and strongest safe ever invented.

However it opened quite easily with a key which was hidden in a secret place known to Lolita.

Her mother's jewels gleamed at her like stars including a diamond necklace with bracelet, ear-rings and a brooch to match, which she knew had cost thousands of pounds. Her stepfather had given them to her mother the first Christmas they were married.

She had played with the jewels like a child with a new toy and now Lolita looked at them quizzically.

She knew that, although her mother had left her everything she possessed in her will, she had no wish to take her jewels.

Then she opened a small drawer which contained a beautiful ring her father had given her mother when they were engaged. It had never been sold however poor they were, although once it had been pawned but only for a few weeks.

It was gold set with three diamonds, not very large, but her mother had always loved it.

Lolita put it on her finger.

Then, as she opened another narrow drawer on the other side of the safe, she gave a little gasp. It was filled with banknotes which she realised could only belong to her stepfather.

She had no scruples about taking what she wanted, although she knew it was stealing in a way.

'If I said I would marry Murdock Tanner,' she consoled herself, 'he would give me this and a hundred times more to buy my trousseau.'

She took two hundred pounds in notes and gold coins, telling herself that by the time it was all spent she would have found employment or someone would befriend her.

She was vaguely thinking at the back of her mind that there was a cousin of her mother's, or a childhood friend, who would be kind to her.

She closed the safe, locked it and put the key back in the drawer and returned to her room.

Fate had been kind and helped her when she most needed it, but it was not going to be easy, in fact the future was likely to be very, very difficult.

At least she was using her brain and if she could not outwit her stepfather, she would only have herself to blame.

'I shall pray,' she thought as she walked into her bedroom. 'And I know God will help me, as he has helped Mama and me in the past.'

She put the money and the ring into her handbag.

She lay on her bed trying to think of where she could go. Her mother's family came from the North and Lolita was sure if she made her way there she would find someone who would remember her as a child.

Her father's family came from the same direction. In fact the original home of the Earls of Walcott and Vernon was only two or three miles from where her mother had lived.

Her father had been educated at Eton and Oxford where he had not particularly distinguished himself. He had then joined the family Regiment, which he had served for two years, leaving because he could simply not afford it.

His father had died and he had inherited the title. He found there were a number of debts which easily swallowed up the money he obtained by selling the ancestral home.

However, he and his wife had been happy in a way which made Lolita's childhood one of colour and love and it was only when she was much older that she had recognised how poor they really were.

'If I go as far away from London as possible,' she now told herself, 'I just hope Step-papa will never be able to find me.'

She was quite certain that he would be determined to pursue her as when he wanted something he never gave up the fight for it.

However, Lolita boasted the blood of the Vernons in her veins. They had fought valiantly for their country and died for it. Yet still they continued to uphold the principles and propriety in which they believed.

'How could I feel anything but degraded if I was married to a man like Murdock Tanner?' Lolita asked herself.

When her lady's maid came to dress her for dinner, she put on one of the prettiest gowns she possessed and added a small string of pearls which her mother, of course with her stepfather's money, had given her the previous Christmas.

"You look lovely tonight, my Lady," the maid said.

"Thank you and I hope it's going to be an enjoyable evening," replied Lolita.

'It will be something to remember,' she thought, 'when perhaps I will have to scrub floors for a living or teach children in one of the village schools now being opened throughout the country.'

She felt that she would be able to earn a living somehow. At least she spoke good English and had a fair knowledge of the ordinary subjects children have to learn at school.

As she descended the stairs she was holding her head high and at the same time her stepfather, wearing his dinner jacket, emerged from the drawing room.

One glance at him told Lolita he had recovered from his bad temper. Now he had got, as he thought, his own way, he was prepared to be conciliatory.

"I hope we will not be late tonight," he said. "I have a very important meeting tomorrow morning and will need all my wits about me."

"I don't think Lady Lansdowne will want to be too late and, as you know, Step-papa, it is one of the parties you asked her to give."

"I have received a note from her, saying there would be twenty people to dinner and another twenty coming in afterwards."

The footman placed his evening cape round his shoulders and he continued,

"There is to be only a small band and I shall be interested to hear what you think of it. Lady Lansdowne says it is one of the best which has appeared this Season and she believes that the Prince of Wales is very pleased with it."

"In which case it must be good," Lolita commented without sounding sarcastic.

She was well aware that everyone wanted to entertain the Prince of Wales and if there was a band that he favoured, it would fly to the top of the tree.

The footman ran the red carpet down the steps and Lolita walked towards the carriage, which was an exceedingly comfortable one drawn by two outstanding horses. They matched each other exactly and were black except for a white star on their noses.

It was the sort of detail for which Lolita had to commend her stepfather, who demanded perfection simply because he could pay for it.

They drove off in silence and then he said,

"I feel sure, as you are a sensible girl, you will have thought over what I said to you."

"I have certainly thought about it, Step-papa."

"Well, that is what I want you to do. Although there is no great hurry, Murdock is not a man to waste time once he has made up his mind."

Lolita did not reply.

They travelled on in silence until just as they arrived at Lady Lansdowne's house, he added,

"Few girls have such possibilities as you. Don't forget that the young men who will flatter you tonight keep a watchful eye on my pocket. At least that will not be the case where Murdock is concerned."

It was the sort of remark that he would make in exceedingly bad taste.

If he had left the subject alone she could have admired him for it, but now she felt her anger rising because of what he had just said.

And terror was again clutching at her like an icy cold hand.

Lolita felt as if she had been trapped and because her stepfather was talking so confidently she realised that he thought there was no fight left in her.

He undoubtedly believed that he had completely won the struggle.

CHAPTER TWO

Lolita woke early and waited until she thought her stepfather had gone down to breakfast before she rang for her maid.

"I'm a little tired after the party last night," she told her, "so I would like breakfast in bed."

It was brought to her about a quarter of an hour later and she was certain that by that time Ralph Piran would have left the house.

Then she got up and when she was dressed she asked the maid to order her a carriage.

"You're going shopping, my Lady?"

"Yes," Lolita answered, "but I don't want anyone with me as I am meeting a friend and having luncheon with her."

She paused and then said as if she had just thought of it,

"I put some dresses in a case yesterday which require a little alteration. It is in the cupboard. Will you take it downstairs and tell the footman to put it in the carriage for me?"

The maid obeyed and Lolita finished dressing.

She had chosen a pretty, but not very spectacular gown. Her hat became her and was not particularly noticeable. The whole outfit was in a soft blue which would not attract attention.

She picked up her handbag containing her mother's ring and the money she had taken from the safe.

She thought later that she would be wise to hide some of the money in the pockets of each of her other garments, so if the money was stolen from her bag she would still have some left.

She then walked along to her mother's room where the blinds were drawn and it was in semi-darkness.

The nurse was elsewhere and so she was alone with her mother.

Lolita knelt down by her bed and prayed fervently that her mother would recover, but she could not help thinking that if she died, she would be with her father and be as happy as they had been when they were together.

Lolita rose to her feet.

Although her mother had not moved since she had knelt beside her, she felt as if in some way she had blessed her and approved what she had decided to do.

Perhaps she was half in the next world already with her father and both of them would understand why she was running away.

She left her mother and walked slowly downstairs.

When the butler bade her good morning, she told him,

"I will not be back for luncheon, in fact I may not be back until dinner-time. I am spending the day with some friends, so I shall not keep the carriage since I know they will bring me home."

The butler nodded and she stepped into the waiting carriage, which was the one she always used when she was going shopping and was drawn by only one horse.

She saw as she sat down that the footman had placed her case on the small seat in front of her and she hoped that she had remembered everything she would require. It would be a mistake to spend any of the money she had brought with her unless she absolutely had to.

She told the footman to drive to the large shop in Bond Street where she usually bought her gowns.

On arrival she sent the carriage away, telling the coachman that a friend would be waiting for her.

As it drove off she had the feeling she was stepping out of one world into another.

The greatest adventure that had ever happened to her had now begun.

The assistant who usually served her came forward smiling and Lolita told her that she required a new evening gown. It was for an important ball she had been invited to next month.

"I cannot wear anything I have worn already," she said. "So I thought you could show me some new designs."

"It'll be a pleasure, my Lady," the assistant replied, looking questioningly at the case Lolita had brought into the shop with her.

"Oh, these are gowns I do not need," she explained, "which I am giving to the friend with whom I am having luncheon. She is organising a sale for one of her pet charities and has assured me that any of the pretty dresses you have made for me will bring in a good sum of money."

"I hope that's true and it's very generous of you, my Lady, to give them anything so valuable."

Lolita laughed.

"I doubt if there is too much value in old clothes, but there is always someone who will benefit by them."

Lolita had been sitting as she was talking to the assistant and now she rose to her feet.

"I want to go out by the door at the side of the shop,which leads into Bruton Street. I am meeting my friend in the shop next door so there is no point in having the carriage wait to carry me such a short distance."

The assistant smiled.

"Your Ladyship thinks of everything," she said flatteringly.

She suggested that one of her staff should carry the case, but Lolita said she would do it herself.

"It really weighs very little and, as I have just said, it is only a short distance."

She said goodbye and then hurried into Bruton Street.

When she was sure she was no longer being watched she saw a Hackney Carriage and hailed it.

"Take me to Illingworth Square," she ordered and the carriage drove off.

As the Square was some distance away, Lolita sat back and thought that she was covering her tracks rather cleverly.

She was sure that when it was discovered that she was missing, her stepfather would at first be angry and then worried. As a last resort, when there was no sign of her, he would undoubtedly engage a detective to discover where she was hiding.

She was determined to make it impossible for anyone to find her.

When they reached Illingworth Square, she paid off the Hackney Carriage.

She had decided that the best course to take would be to find a livery stable where she could hire a chaise to take her out into the country. What was important was that the livery stable should not be anywhere near Berkeley Square and it must not be one likely to be questioned as to whether they had hired a chaise to a young woman looking like herself.

She thought that she should leave the Square by the road which led to the North.

She had just reached the livery stable when a small boy in floods of tears came running from the far end of the Square.

He was running so hard that he bumped into her and Lolita had to put out her hand to prevent him from falling.

"Whatever is the matter? What has hurt you?" she asked.

He looked up at her and she saw that tears were pouring down his cheeks and his hand was bleeding.

"You have cut your hand."

"She beat me – *she beat me*," the boy sobbed. "I have run away – and I am never going back."

It was difficult to hear the words as his voice was hoarse with tears.

Lolita thought she must somehow mop the blood from his hand, if for no other reason to save it soiling her dress.

She looked ahead and saw there was a statue and in front of it a bench.

"Come and sit down", she suggested in a quiet voice, "and I will bind up your hand for you."

The weeping boy walked obediently beside her and his tears were now subsiding and then just as they reached the bench, he looked over his shoulder fearfully.

"They will come and catch me and she will beat me again. I won't go back, *I won't*."

On an impulse which afterwards she thought very strange – it was almost as if she had been directed what to do – Lolita hailed another Hackney Carriage, which had just deposited a passenger and was slowly moving away empty.

"We will drive away," she said to the small boy, "and then they will not be able to catch you."

She opened the door as she spoke and he jumped quickly into the carriage.

"Where do you want to go, ma'am?" the driver asked Lolita.

"This little boy has hurt his hand and I wonder if you could take me to a quiet place where I could bandage it up and perhaps buy him something to drink."

The cabby smiled.

"I knows somewhere as'll suit you."

Lolita climbed in and pulled the door to and they drove off.

"Now tell me who you are," she said to the boy who to her relief had stopped crying.

"I am Simon."

"And who are you running away from?"

"Step-mama," he answered. "She hates me – and she is always beating me. If Papa was alive – he would not let her."

Lolita was looking at his hand, realising that he had been struck several times by a whip and it was one of the weals that was bleeding so profusely.

"Does your stepmother," she asked him quietly "always beat on your hand?"

"She beats my back – and all of me," Simon replied with a sob. "I screams and screams – but she does not stop!"

Lolita felt angry.

If there was one thing she loathed, it was cruelty to children, especially a small child who could not protect himself.

She remembered what her stepfather had said to her in his fury only last night, but she thought it was unlikely he would beat her in the same way as Simon had been beaten and yet he might in fact do anything when he was in one of his rages.

"Now you have run away, where are you going?"

"I am going to my Uncle James. He would not allow Step-mama – to hit me because – he loved Papa."

"And where does your Uncle James live?"

Lolita was beginning to think that she would have to take the small boy there and make his uncle realise how badly he was treated.

"It's a long way," Simon replied slowly, "and I will be very hungry when I get there."

"Tell me where your uncle lives," Lolita persisted, "and perhaps I can help you."

Simon looked at her as if he had just realised she might be helpful in his predicament. Now that he had stopped crying, Lolita saw he was a very good-looking little boy. He had distinguishing features which told her he was born of gentlefolk.

"You have only told me your Christian name. You must tell me your uncle's name, otherwise it will be extremely difficult to find him."

Simon put his hand on his head as if he was thinking. Lolita guessed that he was perhaps seven or not more than eight years old.

She thought he was working out in his mind exactly what she wanted to know and finally he said,

"I am – Simon Brook, but Uncle James – is Lord Seabrook."

Lolita was surprised.

"Lord Seabrook," she repeated, "and you think he would stop your stepmother beating you so cruelly if he knew what was happening?"

"Uncle James loved Papa. He would not allow Step-mama – to be so horrible to me."

"But why does she beat you?" Lolita asked. "Were you being very naughty?"

Simon shook his head.

"She hates me and everything I do is – *wrong.*"

He sounded as though he might cry again, so Lolita said quickly,

"Now you will have to tell me where your uncle lives, otherwise I cannot take you to him."

"You will take me to Uncle James?" Simon asked in an excited voice. "That will be spiffing, and I need never go back to Step-mama."

"Not if he agrees to keep you, but we will have to ask him very nicely to take care of you. Has he any children of his own?"

Simon shook his head.

"No, Uncle James is not married."

"Now where exactly does he live?"

Simon drew in his breath and she knew he was thinking.

"In a castle by a big, big lake," he said. "Papa used to swim in the lake when he was my age."

"Where is the big, big lake?"

"Long, long way."

"Do you know its name?"

"It's a funny name – like an owl," Simon replied.

Lolita looked at him.

"Do you think you mean Ullswater?"

Simon smiled.

"That's right – *Owlswater*. Very big lake – and very big castle. Papa told me all about it."

Lolita felt it was such an extraordinary coincidence that her father's family had lived near Ullswater in the beautiful Lake District in the County of Cumberland.

She had vaguely thought of going there to try to find a cousin or distant relative who would help her in her present predicament. Yet, as she was sure that as none of them was at all well off, she did not wish to encroach on them. She had considered, however, that if she could stay with one of them for a little while, she could decide on what she could do to earn a living – perhaps teaching or looking after children.

All these ideas which had passed through her mind were still distinct possibilities and now by an extraordinary chance this small boy wanted to go in the same direction.

It was then, as she realised that the Hackney Carriage was coming to a standstill, another idea came to her.

If her stepfather was looking for her he would be looking for a young woman on her own and if, as was likely, Simon's cruel stepmother came looking for him, she would be looking for one small boy alone.

So she said to Simon in a very low voice,

"Listen Simon. Because you must hide from your stepmother, I am going to pretend you are my son. So remember, when you speak to me you must call me Mama."

"I want to hide from Step-mama and I want to find Uncle James."

"She may try to prevent you from going to him and therefore no one must tell her where you are, *no one*!"

33

She emphasised her words so that he would understand. And then she added,

"You are disguised and your name is now Bell and I am Mrs. Bell. Do you follow me?"

She thought Simon nodded and next the door opened as the driver had climbed down from his box.

"'Ere you are, ma'am," he said, "and as they be friends o' mine they'll help the little boy where he's 'urt himself."

"You are very kind."

She paid him what he asked for, giving him a tip she thought he would expect. She had learned in the past that it was a great mistake to over-tip anyone as later they remembered who had tipped them and she felt the driver was quite content with her gratitude.

He strode in through the door of what was a small restaurant and shouted for the proprietor.

"'Ere, Bill," he called, "there's a lady with a little boy who's 'urt himself. I says as you'll 'elp 'em."

An elderly man from behind the counter looked up. He did not seem very enthusiastic at what he was being asked to do until he saw Lolita and then as he realised she was 'quality' he was effusively polite.

"Can I 'elp you, ma'am?" he enquired.

"My son has hurt his hand and I would be very grateful if I could just wash the wound before I bandage it."

"'Course, 'course," Bill agreed.

He took them into a room where there was a sink and as it was too early for anyone to come in for luncheon, everything was clean and tidy.

Lolita put Simon's hand under the cold tap and while the water was running on the weals from the sharp whip, Bill produced a bandage.

Lolita thanked him and once Simon's hand was neatly bandaged, she asked if he could have something to drink, perhaps a ginger ale.

Bill produced a bottle and they sat down at a table. He also gave them some chocolate biscuits and Simon ate them with relish.

"What I would like to ask you," said Lolita, "is if there is a livery stable nearby. My son and I need to travel to the country."

"That be an easy question to answer," replied Bill. "There's one just round the corner. It ain't very large like those up West, but you'll find him an honest man, and his 'orses are goin' strong and they'll carry you right enough."

"That is exactly what I want and thank you once again for being so kind."

Lolita paid him for the ginger ale and chocolate biscuits and he refused to take anything for the bandage.

"It's been a pleasure to 'ave you 'ere, ma'am," he said, "and I 'opes you'll come again if you're passin'."

"We will certainly do so," Lolita replied enthusiastically.

She shook his hand as he took her to the door and pointed out the direction of the livery stables.

When they reached the stables, Lolita thought it would be a great mistake to tell the proprietor exactly where they were going.

She therefore told him that their destination was Nottingham which would take at least two days.

"If you can get us halfway there tonight," she said, "I am sure we can find another livery stable if you want your carriage returned."

"I'll send you the whole way, ma'am," said the proprietor, "if you can afford what it'll cost."

Then he told her how much it would be and Lolita thought it seemed very little for the number of miles they had to travel.

However she was not a particularly good judge as she had never had to pay the fees of hired carriages herself. They had always been paid for by her father and for the last two years, since her mother had married Ralph Piran, they had travelled in carriages owned by him.

When Lolita and Simon set off in the Hackney Carriage, she liked the middle-aged man who was the driver and the horse was young, spirited and should not tire too quickly.

The proprietor had advised them where they would be wise to stay the night, but Lolita wanted a small quiet village even though the inn might not be very comfortable.

Finally she agreed to stay at a place which the driver said he knew, and that the inn, though small, was clean and respectable.

As he made his recommendation, he glanced at Lolita and she recognised that he was thinking that she was too young and too pretty to be travelling alone, accompanied only by a small boy.

She had waited until they had set off before she opened her handbag and took out her mother's ring. She had wrapped it in a piece of tissue paper so that it would not be damaged and had placed it carefully at the very bottom of her bag.

Now she slipped it on her finger and turned it round.

When the three diamonds set in it could not be seen, it looked like an ordinary wedding ring.

As they drove off Simon slipped his hand into hers.

"This is so exciting, I hope our horse will go very, very fast."

"If he pulls us too fast at first," Lolita had said, "he will get tired and we have a long way to go before we can stop for the night."

"If we go very fast, Step-mama will not catch us up!"

That was logical, Lolita thought, and for that matter nor would her stepfather.

Although he would not know until tonight that she was missing, it would be a mistake to underestimate his power or his determination.

She was certain that he would be determined to fetch her back and would therefore set into action everything he possessed to get his own way.

'I am sure,' Lolita comforted herself, 'that he will never imagine for a moment I am on my way to Ullswater or that I am accompanied by a small boy who is supposed to be my son!'

To make sure there would be no mistakes, she rehearsed Simon about their disguise.

"I am hiding and you are hiding, Simon. We have to be very clever about it, otherwise I shall be taken back to the house from where I have run away and you will be taken back to your stepmother."

She knew by the quiver which shot through him that he was frightened at the very idea.

37

"We have therefore to be intelligent enough not to make a mistake," Lolita told him, "and I think if anyone asks your age you must say you are six years old."

She knew that she looked very young to have a child of Simon's age and she might have been wiser to say he was her brother.

But in that case, as she was a lady, she would be expected to travel accompanied by a chaperone, but if she was a married woman it was possible for her to be without one.

When they stopped for luncheon, it was at a small inn in a very picturesque village after they had come through a number of larger villages.

The driver had suggested they might like to stop earlier, but Lolita had refused.

In one village there was a horse fair and in another there were signs of a large garden party taking place that afternoon in aid of a local hospital. The next village seemed empty with only the ducks on the pond on the village green to welcome them.

The black and white inn was small but clean and was called the *Queen's Head*.

By this time both Lolita and Simon were hungry and they were provided with a cold luncheon of ham, tongue and a fresh salad from the inn's garden.

Simon ate every one of the strawberries which were brought for their second course, while Lolita enjoyed the local cheese.

Then having washed and tidied themselves they set off again.

Now Lolita had tried to make herself look a little older. She swept back her hair more severely from the side of her small pointed face and arranged it at the back in a way that was not so fashionable or, as she thought, so becoming.

She could not alter her shining eyes or the perfection of her pink and white skin.

If a stranger spoke to her she thought she would frown a little and look reserved and perhaps then they would think she was a responsible married woman rather than a young and excitable girl.

She encouraged Simon to tell her more about his life.

At the end of his story she could put together what she thought was a reliable picture of his family history. She had to invent some of the gaps, but she felt she had very likely guessed correctly.

What she understood was that Simon's father had been the Honourable Rupert Brook, but had married Simon's mother with the disapproval of his grandfather.

They had therefore left Cumberland where Rupert Brook had lived all his life and moved South.

They made new friends and according to Simon were very happy. His father, who was a good rider, bought some young horses which he broke in and sold them for a great deal more than he had paid for them.

Until two years ago when Simon was nearly five years old they had been living contentedly in a small country house in the County of Hertfordshire.

Then unexpectedly Simon's mother died of pneumonia in the winter when it had been very cold and as far as Lolita could understand they had not sent for a doctor as quickly as they should have done.

Both her husband and son were broken-hearted and Rupert Brook felt after she was buried that he could not bear to live in the house where they had been so happy.

Nor could he continue breaking in horses which had provided them with enough money to be comfortably off. He had therefore decided to move to London, where he had taken a small flat for himself and his son while he worked out what he should do.

It was from here that Lolita had to piece together a great deal of what had occurred from the fragments Simon could give her.

What she thought had happened was that Rupert Brook, who was handsome, young and charming, had been pursued by quite a number of beautiful young women and one in particular.

But Simon had never liked her.

She had pretended she loved him and had given him a number of expensive toys and then, if Simon could be believed, she had persuaded his father to marry her, although he still loved his mother.

As she was exceedingly well off, Lolita thought it was perhaps the most sensible thing for him to do.

Then just a year after they were married, Rupert had a fall when hunting with a very well known pack of hounds.

He was jumping a fence and his horse rolled on him. It broke his spine and he died.

His new wife was genuinely upset, but at the same time she had no wish to be hampered with her late husband's son.

Instead of making a fuss of Simon as she had before, she beat him because he annoyed her and found fault with everything he did.

She also tried to get rid of him by writing to his Uncle James who had now inherited the family title. She asked him to take the boy, but the new Lord Seabrook was unmarried and continually travelling, so he replied that it would be best for Simon to stay with her.

She was, according to the boy, furious when she received the letter and beat him unmercifully.

"She hates me – she hates me," Simon cried, "and she wants me to die – like Papa."

"You must try to forget about her,"

Lolita attempted to calm him down. She could not bear him to be upset, so she kissed him and told him a story so that he would not think any more about his stepmother.

Equally she could not help wondering, if her stepfather found her, what she could do about Simon. She knew that she could not abandon him to his stepmother as she was sure that what he had said of her hatred for him was true.

Lolita's conclusion was actually confirmed when they spent the first night in a quiet village at the inn recommended by the owner of the livery stable.

The inn was a little larger than the one they had stopped at for their luncheon. Their two bedrooms were clean and communicated with each other and the meal they ate was plain but well cooked.

When they went up to bed Lolita helped Simon undress. She had noticed during the evening that the shirt he was wearing was sticking to his back.

When she helped him take it off she was horrified at what she saw.

The weals from the whip crossed and recrossed his skin and quite a number of them were bleeding.

She managed to obtain from the inn-keeper's wife a soft cream, which she rubbed very gently onto Simon's back.

As her fingers went over the wounds she became aware that there were others which had already healed. He had not exaggerated when he had said that his stepmother continually beat him.

How anyone could do anything so cruel to a small defenceless child, Lolita could not understand.

She had already found Simon to be good-mannered and well-behaved. His own mother had brought him up well and his father, Lolita thought, had been a real gentleman.

Even to think of a man who was like her own father made her remember how she was menaced by Murdock Tanner.

Perhaps by this time her stepfather would have told him that she had disappeared and the resources of both these ambitious men would be expended on bringing her back.

Later that night when she thought it over more calmly, she doubted if Murdock Tanner really wanted to marry her and additionally it was unlikely that her stepfather would really force her up the aisle, as he had threatened in anger.

It might be advantageous to him where money was concerned for her to be married to such a very rich man, but it certainly would not advance his social ambitions.

What he really wanted, she concluded, was for her to pander to Murdock's interest in her and that she should flirt with him as an older woman would do and not resist his caresses.

The mere idea of him kissing her made Lolita feel sick and she knew that however hard she tried to act the part her stepfather desired, it was impossible for her to even contemplate.

She could not even bear the thought of Murdock even touching her with one finger.

'I hate him, I hate him,' she said to herself, 'and if I have to starve in the gutter, I will not go back. Nothing will make me.'

*

The next morning having slept badly, Lolita was anxious to get away quickly. She wanted to put as many miles between herself and her stepfather as was possible.

When they set off again it was a relief to find the horse was a spirited as it had been the previous day and the driver was just as good-tempered.

Simon said that his back was feeling better and the inn-keeper's wife was kind enough to allow Lolita to buy the pot of cream that had assuaged his wounds for a few pennies.

When they set off it was a sunny morning with just a little freshness in the air and it was exciting to be driving through the twisting country lanes. The hedges were covered with honeysuckle while the fields were golden with buttercups.

They covered about the same distance as the previous day.

They enjoyed a good luncheon and stopped at a small posting inn at about six o'clock. It was like the one they had stayed in last night, but not so comfortable and the food was indifferent and only just edible.

Both Simon and Lolita were glad when they could retire to bed.

She was just drifting off to sleep when she heard Simon scream in the room next door and for a moment she thought she must have imagined it, but then as the sound came again, she jumped out of bed.

Without stopping to put on her dressing-gown she opened the communicating door. She had carefully locked her outer door and Simon's and now she thought someone must have intruded on him.

Then as she reached his bed she could see him in the moonlight coming through the window.

He was still asleep and dreaming.

She put her arms round him and he clutched at her convulsively.

"Save me – save me!" he cried. "Don't let her beat me. Please – *save me!*"

"You are quite safe, Simon," Lolita told him gently,

"Wake up, you are dreaming."

He opened his eyes.

"Oh, it is – you. I thought it was – Step-mama."

"We have left her a long way behind," Lolita assured him.

Simon burst into tears.

"I am frightened. I am so frightened. I thought she had caught up with me and if she does – she will beat me again."

"No one is ever going to beat you again. Listen to me Simon, I promise you I will see that no one hurts you and you must believe me."

She was determined as she spoke that she must prevent this woman somehow from being so cruel to this helpless little boy. Even if it meant her going back to the Social world and ensuring that Mrs. Brook was condemned for her cruelty by every person she knew.

Lolita recognised how gossip could circulate and every time Mrs. Brook appeared, her friends would whisper about her and avoid her.

It was then Lolita remembered that to do this she would have to resume being a *debutante* and socially important with her title as her stepfather desired.

The mere idea made her shiver as so much more was entailed. Yet anything which might happen to her was insignificant compared to everything that Simon had been made to suffer.

Her arms tightened round him as she said soothingly,

"It's all over. You are going to be happy and I promise you that I will never allow you to go back to live with your stepmother again."

As she spoke she was determined that somehow she would force Lord Seabrook into accepting his nephew and if he refused she would look after Simon herself, even though it meant defying her stepfather again.

She felt Simon mover closer to her and knew he was comforted by what she had said.

Very gently she made him lie down on his pillow.

"I am going to tell you a story and while you are listening to it you will fall asleep and have no more nasty dreams."

Lolita smoothed back the hair from his forehead and then bending forward she kissed him gently on each cheek.

"You are just like Mama," murmured Simon, "and I love you."

Lolita kissed him again.

She thought that of all the compliments she had ever received his was the most sincere.

CHAPTER THREE

They took longer to reach Penrith than Lolita had expected, which did not matter except that the journey had cost quite a lot of her money.

She had to buy Simon a new shirt to replace his dirty and blood-stained one as well as a hat to wear if the sun was hot.

They had changed horses twice more and been to yet another livery stable.

Lolita was sure that it would be almost impossible for anyone to follow their tracks.

But now she thought that the big test was still to come as she needed to persuade Simon's uncle to take him in and look after him.

She had already gathered from Simon that Lord Seabrook was young and unmarried and she could quite understand he would feel it very tiresome to have to set up a nursery before he was ready for one.

Equally she was determined that nothing and no one would make her give Simon back to his dreadful stepmother.

When they set off from Penrith to the castle by the lake, she remarked to Simon,

"Now you can be yourself again. You are Simon Brook and I am no longer your mother."

"You are not leaving me?"

There was a note of anxiety in his voice which told her that he was afraid of losing her.

"I don't want to leave you," she told him, "but you must remember that I am in hiding too."

"We will ask Uncle James to hide you," suggested Simon. Lolita thought that was what she was hoping would happen.

"I want to be a governess," she replied, "so perhaps your uncle will allow me to teach you."

"That would be spiffing and I will learn lots and lots, because you tell me such scrumptious stories."

Because she wanted him to sleep and not have to endure any more nightmares, Lolita had told him a story every night when he went to bed.

Then Simon asked her,

"If I am not to call you Mama, what do I call you? What is your name?"

Lolita thought quickly as it was a question which had not occurred to her. "

My name," she said slowly, "is Lo-Lo."

She was trying to find a name like her own which would be easy to remember and she was hovering between Lola and Lorinda.

Simon gave an exclamation.

"Lolo. That is a nice name. I will call you Lolo."

Lolita laughed.

She thought as she was a young governess it would make it easier for him than if he had to call her 'Mrs. Bell.'

"Very well," she said, "I will be Lolo, but do not forget that you have to be very polite to me, because I am a governess!"

Simon put his cheek against her arm.

"I will always be polite to you, Lolo, but not to people who are unkind and cruel to me."

Lolita quickly changed the subject.

They were driving through some particularly beautiful country, when suddenly they caught a glimpse of a huge expanse of water.

"It's *Owlswater*, I know it's *Owlswater*!" cried Simon. "It's just as big as Papa said it would be."

It was certainly a most impressive expanse of water.

The lake seemed to stretch away into a misty distance, which Lolita thought very romantic and at the far end there were tall mountains silhouetted against the sky.

When they drove alongside the lake they saw fields sloping down to the water's edge and there were small boats with coloured sails scattered all over the lake.

Simon was entranced by the view.

"It is just what Papa told me it would be like," he kept saying.

And then suddenly ahead of them Lolita saw the castle.

It was a lovely scene with the sun shining on its battlements with the mountains in the background and she thought the whole scene must have stepped out of a dream.

As they drew nearer still she could see that the castle was very old, but with later additions, and it was now a very imposing building enveloped by trees.

A little later she noticed a beautiful garden filled with flowers sloping down to the lake itself.

It was all so awe inspiring that even Simon was stunned into silence and he just looked around him wide-eyed as they drove up a twisting drive.

Then they were in front of a very impressive porticoed front door with the castle tower on the left side of the great building.

Feeling her heart beating rather quickly, Lolita climbed out of the post-chaise. She paid the driver and thanked him for bringing them safely to their destination.

She picked up her suitcase and taking Simon by the hand they walked up the steps of the castle.

The front door opened before she could pull the bell.

At first she saw two footmen in smart livery and next the butler came forward.

"Is Lord Seabrook at home?" Lolita asked, her voice sounding a trifle nervous.

It had suddenly occurred to her that if he was not at home, they would have to find somewhere to stay until he returned.

To her relief the butler replied,

"His Lordship is in residence, ma'am. May I ask who wishes to see him?"

"Will you please inform his Lordship," answered Lolita, "that I have brought his nephew, Simon Brook, with me?"

The butler gave an exclamation and looked at Simon.

"I knew your father, Master Simon," he said, bending towards the small boy, "and now I sees you resemble him."

"You knew Papa! He told me he lived in this big, big castle."

The butler smiled and said to Lolita,

"Will you please come this way, ma'am?"

He walked ahead and Lolita followed with Simon holding on tightly to her hand. He was looking round excitedly at the great staircase, the huge medieval fireplace and the walls covered with portraits which Lolita was sure were his ancestors.

The butler showed them into an attractive sitting room with windows overlooking the lake.

Letting go of her hand, Simon ran to the window and exclaimed,

"It looks even bigger from here and I can see three boats with white sails."

Lolita looked out as well and she thought that no house could have a more beautiful view, which seemed almost mystic as if it had nothing to do with the ordinary humdrum difficulties of life.

She wondered how Simon's father had ever been able to leave a place so beautiful even though he was in love.

"There's another boat!" enthused Simon. "A bigger one. I want to go in a boat."

"You will have to ask your uncle if he has one. I am sure he has," added Lolita.

As she was speaking the door opened and as she and Simon turned round, she saw a tall and extremely handsome man enter the room.

As he walked towards him, Simon gave a cry of delight.

"Uncle James! Uncle James, I have run away to you."

He threw himself against his uncle, who bent down and put his arms round him.

"This *is* a surprise. No one told me you were coming."

"I ran away because – Step-mama beat me and it hurt so much I cried and cried."

"Beat you?" Lord Seabrook repeated in astonishment.

Simon put out his hand.

"She beat me with a whip, Uncle James, and it bled and bled."

Simon's weals had turned brown, but the one which Lolita had bandaged still showed several ugly scabs.

Lord Seabrook's lips tightened and then he rose and looked towards Lolita.

"What has happened?" he asked. "I imagine you have been kind enough to bring my nephew here to me."

He held out his hand as he spoke and when Lolita's hand touched his, she felt he was both strong and reliable – in fact what she had hoped he would be.

"I brought Simon to you, my Lord, because what he is telling you is the truth. But I think it would be better if we were alone and I can tell you exactly what the situation is."

She thought before they arrived that it would be a mistake to talk too much in front of Simon as she did not want him to remember the terrible state he had been in when she first found him.

He had had another nightmare at the last inn but one where they had stayed on the journey North and she had found that telling him a story before he went to bed prevented him from thinking about his stepmother, but it would take time to heal the mental wounds she had inflicted on him.

Lord Seabrook understood what Lolita was trying to tell him.

"I will tell you what, Simon," he said, "I think as you have driven so far you would like something to drink, and I am sure Barty, my butler, will have some of the chocolates he always kept for me when I was your age."

"I would like that very much," Simon replied.

Lord Seabrook walked to the door and opened it.

Barty could not have been far away and without raising his voice he said,

"I have just told Master Simon that you will give him something nice to drink and some of the chocolates that were always kept for us when his father and I were children."

"I know exactly what you means, my Lord," replied Barty, "and Master Simon be the splitting image of Mr. Rupert when I first comes here."

He came into the room and stretched out his hand towards Simon.

"If you will come with me, Master Simon, I'll show you some exciting things which be hidden in this castle."

"That would be such fun."

Simon was moving towards Barty when he stopped suddenly and turned back towards Lolita.

"You will not go away, Lolo?"

"I will be here when you come back."

"I will bring you a chocolate, if they give me enough."

Lord Seabrook laughed.

"I'm sure they will do so and when you have had a drink and something to eat Barty will bring you back to us."

Simon seemed satisfied and ambled off holding Barty's hand and giving a jump of excitement as he went.

Lord Seabrook closed the door and turned towards Lolita.

"Shall we sit down?" he suggested.

Lolita seated herself on the comfortable sofa and he sat opposite her in an armchair.

"What is all this about my sister-in-law beating Simon," he asked. "I cannot believe she would do such a terrible thing."

"You have seen his hand," replied Lolita quietly, "and his back is very much worse. When I found him, my Lord, there were no less than six weals that were bleeding and I could see he had been beaten many times."

"I cannot believe it!" exclaimed Lord Seabrook.

"How could anyone do anything so brutal?"

"That is just what I thought myself," answered Lolita. "So when he told me he had run away I brought him to you."

"That is exactly what you should have done, but how did you meet Simon?"

Lolita smiled.

"I happened to be in Illingworth Square when he bumped into me because he could see nothing through his tears. He told me he had run away and when I realised he was serious and saw the way he had been treated, I knew it would be wrong to try and persuade him to go back to his stepmother."

"Of course it would have been," agreed Lord Seabrook, "and I am extremely grateful to you. But how did you travel here all the way from London?"

"By post-chaise and quite a number of them."

"They must have cost you quite a lot and of course I will refund all your expenditure."

"Thank you, my Lord," said Lolita. "I would have spent it willingly, but as it happens I am at the moment looking for employment as a governess."

"As a governess?"

The way he looked at her told Lolita without words that he thought she did not look in the least like a governess.

She was wearing the dress she had run away in, which had obviously come from an expensive shop and she was sure that he was astute enough to know it was too smart for anything that an average governess could afford.

"You sound surprised," said Lolita quickly, "but what I have told you is the truth. I have to earn my living and I think Simon is very happy with me as I do understand how to keep him from dwelling on his past suffering. So I am hoping I might perhaps stay with him."

She had no idea how lovely she looked as she gazed at Lord Seabrook pleadingly.

He was not only astounded but somewhat suspicious as to why she wished to be a governess.

A dozen questions came to his lips, but aloud he said,

"Of course I should be delighted if you would stay with Simon, at any rate until I can decide what will be best for him. I have been rather remiss in not yet asking your name."

He smiled before he added,

"I heard Simon call you Lolo, which I thought was an affectionate name but not particularly authoritative."

"My name is Bell, my Lord, and I am a widow."

She thought Lord Seabrook looked a little surprised when she uttered the last word. "

My husband was killed in an accident," she continued, "after we had been married only for a very short time and as I now have very little money I have to earn my living."

"I understand and of course it would be extremely convenient for me if you looked after Simon at any rate until he has completely recovered from the intolerable way he has been treated."

"That is what has been worrying me, my Lord, and he has had several very bad nightmares, but I have discovered that telling him a story before he goes to sleep prevents him from thinking that his stepmother will pursue him."

She clasped her hands together as if to make Lord Seabrook understand as she resumed, "

All the way here Simon was afraid she was following us and would find us before we could reach you. It is a very real fear for him! I am sure you will appreciate that it will take some time before he forgets what has occurred and is no longer afraid of being captured again."

Lolita did not realise that there was a little tremor in her voice. She was thinking it was not only Simon who would be afraid of capture but herself as well.

There was silence for a moment and then Lord Seabrook said, "

I can assure you, Mrs. Bell, that I am delighted for you to stay here and teach Simon that all human beings are not as cruel as his stepmother."

He drew in his breath before he added,

"How could I imagine for one moment that she would behave in such an appalling manner?"

"Simon said that she hated him," responded Lolita, "and perhaps it was because when your brother died she had no children of her own. I have often read in stories, although I have not met it in real life, that step-parents are almost fanatically jealous of their partners' children because they are not their own."

Lord Seabrook nodded.

"I have read the same stories and now it has happened to us in real life we shall have to do something about it."

"I thought you would understand, my Lord," said Lolita, "and thank you for saying I can stay with Simon. It matters more to me than I can possibly tell you."

She thought as she spoke that she had been somewhat indiscreet. The words had come impulsively to her lips.

Then before Lord Seabrook could speak again the door opened and Simon came rushing in.

"I've had a scrumptious drink, Lolo," he called, running to Lolita's side, "and here's a chocolate for you. They are delicious and I've eaten three."

He gave Lolita a chocolate wrapped up neatly in some pretty paper.

"That is most kind of you, but I think I will keep it until I am hungry."

"I am hungry now," Simon piped up, "and Barty says luncheon is ready now."

"Then of course we must go into the dining room" said Lord Seabrook, rising to his feet. "But I expect Mrs. Bell would like to wash her hands first, so you and I will wait here while Barty takes her up to Mrs. Shepherd."

He walked to the door and they could hear him giving instructions to Barty.

Simon slipped his hand into Lolita's.

"It's fabulous here," he bubbled. "Very big and exciting. There's armour in the passage and they look like real soldiers!"

Lolita thought that might have been expected in an ancient castle. She walked towards the door and found Barty waiting to take her upstairs.

"You come with me, Simon," said Lord Seabrook, "and I will show you one or two of the family treasures while we are waiting."

Simon went off with him excitedly and Lolita started up the stairs.

The housekeeper, rustling in black silk with a chatelaine at her waist, was waiting at the top for her.

"I'm Mrs. Shepherd, ma'am," she introduced herself, "and I understand you'd like to wash your hands before luncheon."

"Yes, that is just what I would like to do," replied Lolita, "and I think I might take off my hat as well."

"That'll be more comfortable," agreed Mrs. Shepherd, "and, as I always says myself, more homely."

She went ahead and showed Lolita into a room on the first landing.

"If you're staying with Master Simon," said Mrs. Shepherd, "I'll have the schoolroom ready for you. It just happens I had all the rooms on the second floor turned out last week. It seems as if fate was telling me they'd be needed!"

"It's very nice for Simon to come to the castle," commented Lolita, "which he had heard so much about from his father."

A housemaid came hurrying in with a can of hot water which she placed on the washstand.

Lolita took off her hat sitting in front of a mirror surrounded by golden cupids placed on a very elaborate dressing table.

The bed had a carved and gilt canopy and the furniture, Lolita thought, was just what she might have expected to find in such an impressive castle.

Knowing that she should not keep luncheon waiting, she hurriedly tidied her hair, hoping it made her look older than she was.

Then having washed her hands she thanked Mrs. Shepherd for looking after her.

"It's been a pleasure, ma'am, and if his Lordship doesn't need you after luncheon, I'll show you the schoolroom."

"I would like that very much and thank you again."

Lolita hurried down the stairs to find Simon inspecting yet another suit of armour in the passage and Lord Seabrook was telling him the story of the battles which had been fought by his ancestors with some of the trophies they had brought back with them displayed proudly in the hall.

When Simon saw Lolita he came running towards her holding out his arms.

"This is a such an exciting castle, just like your stories and I want to explore it from the top of the tower down to the dungeons."

"I am sure you will be able to see everything before long," Lolita told him, "but I think your uncle is hungry."

"I think we are keeping my other guest waiting," remarked Lord Seabrook.

Lolita wondered who it was and then he opened a door beside them and walked ahead into a very attractive and exquisitely furnished drawing room.

Seated in an armchair in front of the fireplace was a woman.

It had never occurred to Lolita that Lord Seabrook might have guests staying at the castle and she thought she had been rather stupid in expecting him to be on his own.

The woman in the armchair held out a slim-fingered right hand.

She said in what seemed a caressing and somewhat seductive voice,

"I thought you had forgotten all about me."

"How could I possibly forget you?" replied Lord Seabrook soothingly. "But as it happens I have had an unexpected visitor."

"A visitor!" exclaimed the woman.

"My nephew, poor Rupert's son, and I am delighted to have him here."

He put out a hand and pulled Simon forward as he spoke.

"Simon," he said, "this is a very beautiful lady, in fact the most beautiful lady in the whole of London. She has been kind enough to come North and stay with me. Her name is Lady Cressington."

Simon held out his hand and Lady Cressington said in a rather affected tone,

"Oh, what a dear little boy. I'm sure he has a likeness to you."

It was a pleasant enough remark, but Lolita was quite certain it was completely insincere.

She did not quite know why she should think so, yet there was a note in Lady Cressington's voice which told her that she was not at all pleased to see Simon or anyone else.

Lolita was sure that she wished to be alone with her host.

Lord Seabrook turned back.

"And I must introduce Mrs. Bell, who has kindly brought Simon to me and is going to stay with him as his governess."

Lady Cressington gave Lolita a brief and indifferent nod and then having glanced at her without any interest she looked again and her eyes widened.

"A governess! I should have thought your nephew was old enough for a tutor."

"We will think about that later," said Lord Seabrook, speaking as if he thought she was being rather rude to Lolita.

Then before there could be any reply Barty announced,

"Luncheon is served, my Lord."

Lady Cressington held out her hand again and Lord Seabrook helped her rise to her feet.

She was slim and sinuous and was wearing an extremely elaborate gown in a somewhat startling shade of pink. She was also bedecked with more jewellery than Lolita thought was appropriate for the country.

Ignoring Lolita completely she walked towards the door with Lord Seabrook at her side and Simon followed them.

Then as if instinctively he realised Lolita was being ignored, he slipped his hand into hers.

"The castle's full of treasures, Lolo," he said.

"We will explore them all when we get the chance," Lolita assured him.

As they walked towards the dining room they went down a high-ceilinged passage filled with all kinds of interesting objects, including a wall of swords and ancient rifles arranged around a shield.

Lolita could understand that any little boy would be thrilled at everything in the castle and she thought history would be a very easy subject to teach in such surroundings.

The dining room was large and must in ancient times have been the banqueting hall. There were magnificent crystal chandeliers and a marble mantelpiece, which must have been carved by one of the great craftsmen of the eighteenth century.

Lady Cressington continued to ignore both Simon and Lolita.

She flirted with Lord Seabrook in the accomplished manner that Lolita had seen the married ladies using in London.

It was, she thought, like watching a clever performance on the stage and she only wondered if Lord Seabrook realised how artificial it really was.

He laughed at Lady Cressington's innuendos and her *double entendres*, which she often spoke in French as if she thought Lolita would be ignorant of that language.

Simon was hungry and had no wish to chatter and by the end of the meal Lolita had become well aware of exactly what her position would be as a governess.

Lord Seabrook spoke to her only once or twice and every time he did so Lady Cressington deliberately turned the subject to something personal or alternatively she answered the question he had asked before Lolita could do so.

Luncheon was just finished when Barty came to Lord Seabrook's side to say,

"Excuse me, my Lord, Mr. Winter wishes to have a word which I thinks concerns your Lordship's yacht."

"Oh, yes, of course, it is being brought here today and I told Winter where I wanted it anchored."

"Is a yacht a ship?" asked Simon excitedly. "Have you a ship all of your own, Uncle James?"

"I have, indeed, and as soon as it is seaworthy I will take you on it."

"I would like that so very much," enthused Simon. "Can I stand on the bridge and help you drive it?"

Lord Seabrook laughed.

"You shall certainly try, but I shall be very angry if you run it ashore or into a rock!"

"I will never do that, I just want to go to sea in a big ship."

"I am afraid we cannot oblige you with the sea," said Lord Seabrook, "but the lake is there and we will explore it together."

"It's a big, big lake, just like Papa told me."

"There is another big lake near it and I am sure you will enjoy our voyages of discovery."

He looked at Lolita as he spoke the last words and she commented,

"Which could certainly be part of Simon's education."

"That is just what I thought," agreed Lord Seabrook.

He had risen to his feet as he was speaking and when he reached the door he said,

"I will join you as quickly as I can in the drawing room unless you want to go into the garden."

It was not exactly obvious whether he was speaking to Lady Cressington or Lolita.

"Let us go down to the lake," suggested Simon.

"We will certainly do so, but perhaps we should wait until your uncle comes back, because he may want to take you himself."

"I will run and ask him."

Without waiting he ran across the room and out of the door after Lord Seabrook and he was too quick for Lolita to stop him.

For the moment there was no one else in the room.

Lady Cressington rose from her chair and in a sharp aggressive voice which was very different from the one she had been using with Lord Seabrook, she said,

"I suppose you know, Mrs. Bell, that it is usual if governesses do come down for luncheon that they are seen and not heard. What is more I consider that Simon is old enough to go to school and the sooner his Lordship finds the right place for him, the better it will be for the child."

"I am afraid I must disagree with you," replied Lolita. "Simon has been through a very difficult and unhappy experience, which is why I have brought him to his uncle. It is absolutely essential for him to take things easy until he no longer remembers what has upset him in the past."

"That may be your opinion," insisted Lady Cressington, "and of course you want to keep your job. But you are too young to be a governess and, as I have already said, the boy should be at school with other boys of his own age."

As she finished speaking she walked towards the door and left the dining room.

It was then that Lolita realised that having rescued Simon from a life of misery she might have to rescue him again.

She could not believe it was possible.

Yet at the same time Lady Cressington was exceedingly beautiful and it was quite obvious that she was courting Lord Seabrook, if that was the right word for it. Doubtless with the intention of marrying him.

Vaguely at the back of her mind Lolita remembered that she had seen Lady Cressington before. It was at one of the balls she had attended in London and for the moment she could not remember which one it was.

She was certain that Lady Cressington had been pointed out to her as one of the great beauties of the Season.

As far as she could recall she had been surrounded by a number of admiring young men.

She was certainly beautiful, but the difference in her tone of voice when she spoke to Lord Seabrook or to her was a revelation.

'She is here alone and un-chaperoned,' thought Lolita, 'so she can only be thinking of becoming the Mistress of the castle.'

If her conclusion was true, it was a frightening prospect for Simon and yet Lolita was almost sure that was the reason why she wanted to push Simon out and of course her.

The boy came back to say that his uncle was not certain how long he would be and therefore he thought it a good idea if Mrs. Bell took him down to the lake.

They set off hand in hand with Lolita thinking there was no need for her to put on her hat as the sunshine was warm but not too hot.

Simon was thrilled when having passed through the garden, they came to the lake.

He threw stones and because he was so excited at being on the edge of the water, Lolita let him take off his shoes and socks and paddle, but telling him to be careful with his clothes.

"We have not found out yet," she cautioned, "if there are any clothes here for you to wear. If you get these dirty or wet, you will have to stay in bed."

She was only joking, but Simon responded,

"I'm not going to stay in bed while there is a castle to explore. I expect Uncle James owns a lot of horses."

Lolita remembered that Simon's father had loved horses and so she suggested that they visit the stables.

It was difficult to draw Simon away from the lake, but she managed it in the end and they found the stables were, as he had expected, filled with horses and when she introduced Simon to the head groom, he said he remembered Mr. Rupert.

He lifted Simon on to one of the largest stallions so that he could see how tall it was and Simon was thrilled with everything.

"I would love to ride this horse," he told the head groom. "I'll have to ask 'is Lordship to find you somethin' a little smaller than this stallion, Master Simon. As it 'appens I knows where there's a pony for sale which'll be just the right height for you."

"I am sure Simon would love it," added Lolita. "I expect he will be a good rider, as it runs in the family."

"He couldn't be anythin' else," the head groom said, "with 'is Lordship lookin' as if he were born on a horse, and you'd 'ave said the same of Mr. Rupert."

When they returned to the castle Lord Seabrook was looking for them.

"I wondered what had happened to you," he began. "I went to the lake and wondered if you had fallen in."

"I paddled," Simon told him. "It was rather cold for my feet and the stones were slippery. Lolo was frightened I would fall in because she said if I did, as I have no clothes to wear, I would have to stay in bed, so we went to the stables."

"That was a very wise thing to do."

Turning to Lolita he asked,

"Is it true that he has no other clothes?"

"Nothing except what he stands up in, my Lord, and a new shirt I bought for him."

"We must talk to Mrs. Shepherd," proposed Lord Seabrook. "I am sure she has an Aladdin's cave filled with the clothes my brother and I used to wear. In fact at times she has even produced items which belonged to my grandfather and my great-grandfather!"

Lolita laughed.

"That is where you are lucky in owning a castle big enough for everything. Most people have to clear out their attics before they buy anything more than a new pair of shoes."

"What about you?" he enquired of Lolita. "I understand you have brought only one small case between the two of you."

"I expect I shall be able to manage, my Lord. At any rate while it is still summer."

"It depends what you want to do. If Simon wants to ride, I rather suspect you will want to ride with him."

"Why do you think that, my Lord?" asked Lolita curiously.

"I don't know," he answered. "I just thought you would like to ride on a horse. Am I wrong?"

"I have been riding since I could crawl and if I could ride with Simon it would be wonderful. It would be something I would rather do more than anything else in the world!"

"Then of course your wish is granted," Lord Seabrook told her, "and I am sure you will find my horses as good, if not better, than anything you have ridden in the South."

"You are so very kind, my Lord," said Lolita. "I hoped and prayed you would be and I am very grateful that my prayers have been answered."

She spoke with the sincerity which told him she was speaking the truth.

At the same time she had no idea how curious he was, wondering how he could find out more about her.

'How is it possible,' he asked himself, 'that anyone so beautiful, so well-dressed and obviously a lady in the full sense of the word, should pick up an ill-treated little boy crying in the street, and to bring him without asking anyone the long distance from London to Ullswater to save him from a cruel and unpleasant stepmother?'

What was more, this lovely girl, for she was little more, had said she was a widow.

Yet his instinct told him that she was innocent and untouched.

She was certainly not besmirched by the gentlemen in London, who pursue relentlessly any female so stunning if she was not heavily chaperoned.

'I do not understand,' Lord Seabrook said to himself.

He recognised that she was a puzzle and he was determined to find the answer, and he would not be satisfied until he had.

CHAPTER FOUR

Lolita and Simon spent an exciting afternoon exploring the castle.

Several times Lord Seabrook was called away, but they continued on their own.

It certainly was the most fascinating castle Lolita had ever seen, but, as she told herself, she had not seen very many.

She returned with Simon to the schoolroom, which she found was even pleasanter than she had expected.

The room itself was large and in a cupboard they found a number of toy soldiers which Simon's father and uncle had obviously played with when they were boys.

Simon was entranced with it all.

Lolita thought the bedrooms were very comfortable and the larger, Mrs. Shepherd said, was for her, while the smaller one on the other side of the schoolroom was more appropriate for Simon.

"It's where his father slept," she said, "and I feel he'll like the pictures which haven't been changed all the years the room has been empty."

Simon was happy to be anywhere as long as he was with Lolita, who realised he was always looking for her. Although he was quite happy to go a little way with someone else, he always came back to her.

It was as if he thought that he belonged with her.

She considered that more fresh air would be good for Simon, so they walked down to the lake again.

Simon threw more stones and Lolita showed him how to make them skim. Then they walked back for tea which was laid out for them in the schoolroom.

Lolita remembered that a governess usually had luncheon with her employers because the children were present and for dinner she would be alone in her glory in the schoolroom.

Lolita therefore was not surprised when Lord Seabrook sent for Simon after tea and the footman announced,

"His Lordship wants to say goodnight to Master Simon." There was no suggestion of her going too and Lolita waited in the schoolroom until Simon returned.

He came back full of excitement.

"Uncle James says he has a pony coming for me tomorrow and I'll learn to ride it."

"Have you not ridden before?"

"I rode one of Papa's horses sometimes, but when he died we lived in London and there were no horses."

He sounded sad about it which Lolita thought was a good sign and she was sure it was very important that Simon should enjoy riding like his father and his uncle.

She had not forgotten that Lord Seabrook had said that she could ride too. She was looking forward to it eagerly, but at the same time she was very conscious that she had not brought a riding habit with her.

It had been a long day and she put Simon to bed early and he was asleep almost before she left him.

When she went into the schoolroom it was to find Mrs.Shepherd waiting for her.

"I was hoping to see you," said Lolita, "because his Lordship said you might have some clothes for Simon. He only has what he stands up in, and I had to buy a new shirt for him as his was so stained with blood."

"I've been hearing how wickedly that woman treated him," Mrs. Shepherd answered. "I could not believe anyone who calls herself a lady would behave in such a manner."

"I agree with you it was appalling and that is why it is very important for Simon to have new interests so that he will forget what he has suffered."

"It's nice for us to have him here," said Mrs. Shepherd, "and I hope it'll take his Lordship's mind off the lady who seems intent on staying for ever."

Lolita thought this was a rather strange remark, but she wanted to keep Mrs. Shepherd's mind on what she required.

"His Lordship was gracious enough to say that I might ride with Simon, but you understand that as I came away in a hurry I have no riding habit."

Mrs. Shepherd laughed.

"I can find you one right enough. And as you're so slim there'll be no difficulty."

"That is very kind of you."

"I tell you what we'll do. We'll go and find one now, just in case his Lordship wants you to ride tomorrow morning. He usually goes out early."

Lolita thought this was unlikely, but equally she was anxious to locate a suitable riding habit.

Mrs. Shepherd took her up to the third floor and the attics and she said that as the castle was so big they were used only for storage.

"My housemaids are very comfortable in the West wing," she told Lolita, "and Mr. Barty has plenty of room downstairs for his footmen."

There was a note of pride in the way she spoke and Lolita sensed she was not only fond of the castle, but felt she belonged to it.

Her mother had often told her how servants in an ancestral house often think of it as their own home. It belonged to them hardly less than it belonged to its owners.

"That is why, dearest," her mother had said, "we always had such wonderful servants at home."

"It must have hurt Papa to have to sell Walcott Priory."

"It made him very unhappy," her mother had replied. "But there was no money and as it is so large, it was quite impossible for us to keep it up."

She gave a little sigh before she added,

"Your grandfather left a great number of debts which had to be paid."

In the attic there were many wardrobes and numerous clothes on hangers suspended from the walls and covered with white sheets.

Mrs. Shepherd knew exactly what she wanted and eventually she found a large amount of boy's clothes for Simon which Lolita was sure would fit him. There were also riding boots and a smart suit he could wear on important occasions.

Mrs. Shepherd laid them all out on chairs and said she would send one of the footmen to bring them down to the schoolroom.

"Now Mrs. Bell," she turned to Lolita, "we must think about you," as they moved into yet another attic room.

There, Lolita found, were a variety of clothes which had been handed down over the generations. There were wedding dresses which had been worn up to two hundred years ago and a number of fancy dresses which had clearly been a sensation at some special ball and never worn again.

Mrs. Shepherd next went to another wardrobe and when she opened the door Lolita saw it was filled with ladies' riding habits.

Some were pretty but quite out of date as habits had become more tailored and not ornamented with as much braid as they had been earlier in the century.

The one which Lolita liked the most was dark blue and she was sure it would fit her.

She tried on the coat and found she was right as it fitted her almost as if it had been made for her and looked as if it had hardly been worn.

"That one belonged to his Lordship's mother," Mrs. Shepherd informed her. "She was very extravagant where clothes were concerned and I understand his Lordship, her husband, complained that she cost him more than his best horses!"

"I expect she must have been very beautiful," sighed Lolita.

"You'll see pictures of her in the castle, and then you'll know when you see the portrait of his Lordship's father where the young ones gets their looks."

"Simon will be just as good-looking when he is grown up."

"What he needs," remarked Mrs. Shepherd, "is children of his own age to play with, but I thinks they be few and far between in this part of the country."

"Perhaps his Lordship will soon have a family," added Lolita lightly.

To her surprise Mrs. Shepherd made an exclamation of horror.

"I hope not indeed," she said, "not with that lady as is downstairs doing her best to march him up the aisle."

"Do you mean Lady Cressington?"

"Who else?" spluttered Mrs. Shepherd. "She comes here uninvited and his Lordship's too kind and hospitable to tell her she's overstayed her welcome!"

"Perhaps he enjoys having her to stay," suggested Lolita.

"*That's what I'm afraid of.*"

Then as if Mrs. Shepherd felt she was saying too much, she suddenly closed the wardrobe door and said,

"We'll take that habit down for you to try on, Mrs. Bell, and if it doesn't fit, I'll come back for another."

Lolita realised from the way Mrs. Shepherd spoke that even discussing Lady Cressington made her feel angry. Again it seemed strange but she was too tactful to press the subject.

They talked about other things and Lolita had another look at the fancy dresses before they went back to the schoolroom.

She peeped in at Simon and saw that he was fast asleep with a faint smile on his lips.

She thought that tonight it was unlikely he would have another nightmare, although she had not told him a story. Just the same, as their rooms were not next to each other, she left his door into the schoolroom open.

There was another door on the other side of the room which opened into her bedroom and she knew that if he cried or was unhappy she would hear him.

She was very tired after such an eventful day, but she could not resist trying on the riding habit before she went to bed and found that Mrs. Shepherd had been right. It fitted her as if it had been made for her.

She thought too she looked very smart in it and there was a hat to go with it and riding boots which had been brought downstairs for her.

'How could I have been so lucky?' Lolita asked herself as she climbed into bed.

It was a large bed and very comfortable.

She thought God had been very kind in bringing Simon into her life when she had run away.

It never struck her, looking as she did, that she might have been dangerously involved with men. She had only thought that it would be difficult for her to find anywhere to go and even more difficult to secure employment.

It was only now she remembered that she should have written herself a reference, but if she had gone to an agency, they would have thought she was far too young to be a governess or even a teacher in a school.

As she said her prayers she thanked God for looking after her and not letting her suffer for being rather stupid.

'I should have thought it all out more carefully,' she told herself.

Then because she was really very tired she fell into a dreamless sleep.

*

She was woken by the sun coming through the sides of the curtain.

Remembering where she was and how beautiful the lake had been, she jumped out of bed and looked out of the window.

Ullswater Lake was even lovelier than it had seemed yesterday when it had been a little misty over the mountains. Now the sun was shining brightly on the water and the birds were flying below in the garden.

'I must go out,' Lolita decided. 'I cannot waste even a moment of this glorious day.'

At that very moment there was a knock on the door and when she crossed the room to open it she found a housemaid outside.

"Excuse me, ma'am," she said. "His Lordship asks if you'd like to ride with him. He says he'll be ready in twenty minutes and there'll be a pony for Master Simon."

"Please tell his Lordship I would love to ride with him and Simon," replied Lolita effusively.

She ran into the schoolroom and into Simon's room. He was awake and just as she had done he was gazing out of the window in delight.

"There are no boats," he complained as came in.

"It's too early for them, but your uncle has just sent a message that there is a pony waiting for you in the stables."

Simon gave a hoot of joy.

"Hurry up and dress," Lolita urged him, "and I will help you as soon as I have put my clothes on."

She ran back to her own room and then she heard the maid, who Mrs. Shepherd had told her had been allocated to the schoolroom, come in through the other door.

She asked her to help Simon, while she dressed herself as quickly as she could.

Not only did the riding habit fit her, but so did the riding boots which were short as had been fashionable thirty years earlier. Lolita knew that some of the ladies who rode in Rotten Row now wore higher boots like the men.

The pair that had belonged to Simon's grandmother were comfortable enough, if just a trifle large, which was far better, Lolita thought, than if they had been too tight.

She was dressed and her hair was tidied under her hat as she went next door to find that the housemaid had dressed Simon and he was jumping about with excitement.

"I want to see my pony," he piped up as Lolita joined him. "It's so thrilling to have a pony all of my own!"

"You must thank your uncle very much for being so kind," Lolita told him.

"I'll not forget. He's a very nice uncle."

"Very nice indeed," agreed Lolita.

They walked downstairs hand in hand.

It was actually a few minutes before the time his Lordship had asked for them and he was in the hall as Lolita and Simon reached the bottom of the stairs.

"You are very punctual," he said with a hint of surprise in his voice.

"How can we be anything else when it is all so exciting, my Lord." Lolita replied.

"Lolo says you have a pony for me, Uncle James," said Simon, "and I am to say thank you very, very much."

"Better wait and see it first in case you don't like it."

"I have always wanted a pony of my own, but Papa died before he could give me one."

"Well, let's go and see what your pony looks like."

Lord Seabrook walked towards the door with Lolita and Simon following him.

When they went outside the horses were coming from the stables each one led by a groom.

Lolita saw that Lord Seabrook was going to ride the big stallion she had admired yesterday and the horse intended for her was an elegant bay that she could see at a glance was exceedingly well-bred.

Behind them there came a piebald pony and Simon gave a cry of joy and ran towards it.

"How could you have found one so quickly, my Lord?" asked Lolita.

Lord Seabrook smiled.

"As a matter of fact its owner has been badgering me to buy it for some time. It has won several prizes for its appearance and style, but he now wants to move South and hoped I would take over this pony and two other horses in his stable."

"It is exactly what I wanted Simon to have," Lolita told him. "If anything will make him forget what he has been through, it will be having a pony of his own."

"I thought that too and he must also have a dog. If there is anything which prevents a man of my age from thinking about himself, it is having an animal to care for."

Lolita thought this was a very intelligent remark.

"I think," she said, "it is wonderful of you and I cannot tell you how grateful I am."

"You talk as if Simon is your own son."

"I wish he was, my Lord. I hope one day I shall have one just as nice and as handsome."

Lord Seabrook's eyes twinkled and he lifted her onto the saddle of the bay.

He did not ask her if he should do so and as he put his hands on her small waist, Lolita felt a strange feeling run through her.

It was certainly not the revulsion she had felt for Murdock Tanner and she told herself it was because she felt rather shy.

Simon was already astride his pony and Lord Seabrook mounted his stallion and led the way.

Behind the castle there was a field of grass and at the far end a small copse and they all three rode slowly across it.

The groom who was leading Simon was almost running as he held the leading rein.

Lolita was delighted to see that the little boy seemed quite at home in the saddle and was obviously not in the least nervous.

As they reached the copse at the end of the field, Lolita could see the way through the trees and there were more fields on the other side.

Lord Seabrook reined in his stallion that was bucking a little to show his independence and was clearly very fresh.

He led the way through the woods and as they reached the field beyond he said to Lolita,

"I suggest, Mrs. Bell, we give our horses their heads. Simon can follow us more slowly, or rather as fast as the groom leading him can run."

Lolita smiled because she had already heard Simon say he wanted to go faster and faster.

"I think that is an excellent idea, my Lord," she replied. "Let me just explain to Simon what we are doing."

She turned her horse round.

"Simon, your uncle and I are going to gallop our horses because they are fresh and need a good run. When you have had more practice, you will be able to gallop with us. Today you cannot go so fast, but we will be coming back with you."

"I want to go as fast as you," called Simon.

"I expect in a short while you will be going faster still," Lolita told him, "but you must understand that you have to get to know your pony first."

"I like him very much and he likes me!"

"Then just take him gently and talk to him as you do so. Then he will understand what you want."

She rode back to Lord Seabrook and was aware that he had overheard what she had said.

As she reached him he commented,

"I see you know a great deal about horses and even more about small boys."

"I think both are very lovable and I can see, as I am sure you can, my Lord, that Simon will in time become as good a rider as his relatives."

"Which of course delights me. Now are you ready?"

Lord Seabrook smiled at her before he touched his stallion gently and he was off immediately at a gallop.

Lolita's horse was not to be outdone and in a few seconds they were racing each other.

While Lolita knew he was bound to win, she was determined to give him a good run for his money and her horse felt the same.

When they had ridden for over a mile and Lord Seabrook pulled up, Lolita was only just a whisker behind him.

"I was right," he said, as she drew her bay to a standstill.

"In what way?"

"You not only ride exceptionally well, but you look very lovely on horseback."

Lolita's eyes widened with surprise and then she laughed.

"You are very kind, my Lord, and I know that few people would be so hospitable to a governess."

"Let me say," he remarked, "that few governesses look like you or ride like you!"

"I do not believe, my Lord, that you have met many governesses, not having any children of your own."

"When I do have them, I hope they are like Simon, who I think is an exceptionally charming little boy."

"He is so exceptional," agreed Lolita, "that I was very frightened before I came here that you might not understand."

"And now I do?" Lord Seabrook questioned.

"I am so very grateful, my Lord, and I never thought I should be so lucky as to ride such a marvellous horse as this one."

She bent forward to pat her bay as she was speaking.

Watching her Lord Seabrook thought that no one would believe for a moment that she was a governess unless they were blind. Nor that she had ever been forced to earn her own living.

'There is some deep mystery behind all this,' he thought. 'I must persuade her to trust me and tell me the truth.'

He knew, however, that to press her would be like jumping a fence too quickly, so he just remarked,

"I always enjoy riding before breakfast because the air is fresh and there is something very magical about a new day."

"Everything here is magical," Lolita enthused. "When I first saw the lake yesterday I thought I must have stepped out of a dream."

"I have often thought that myself and it was certainly very sensible of my ancestors to build their castle here on Lake Ullswater."

They rode back to collect Simon.

They were then approaching the castle from another direction when Lolita asked,

"What is that building I can see to the North which is rather higher than the ground around it?"

"Oh, that is Walcott Priory. With the exception of the castle it is the oldest building in the County. For hundreds of years it was a Priory for Benedictine monks."

Lolita gasped inaudibly beneath her breath, staggered that she had at last found her father's ancestral home, and she could see that it looked most impressive and was sure that because it was so old it would be even more beautiful if one was closer to it.

"Who lives in the Priory?" she enquired nervously.

"The late Earl with whom the title died out," Lord Seabrook told her, "sold it to a man who had made a lot of money in the cotton business. He found the house too big for him and at the moment it is empty."

"I would be interested to see it sometime, my Lord," said Lolita, trying to speak casually, "and of course I must tell Simon about the monks."

"That is an excellent idea. The castle is full of the history which he will have to learn about sooner or later."

"I shall make sure that he enjoys every word of it, as I have always found history fascinating myself."

They rode on for a little while before Lord Seabrook unexpectedly asked her,

"Have you ever been abroad?"

"Yes, indeed I have, I have been to France, Italy and Greece."

Lolita's father and mother had saved every year so that they could have what they called 'a second honeymoon' abroad.

When they found it impossible to leave her behind, she had gone with them. There had always been someone in a small *pension* who would look after her when they went out in the evening.

In the daytime she remembered playing on the beaches and staying by a river while her father and mother talked to each other in loving terms, as if they had just met for the first time.

"I suppose your travelling makes you even more qualified to be a governess than you would be otherwise?"

"My French is pretty good, while my Italian is a little spasmodic, but in Greece I preferred what I saw to what I heard."

Lord Seabrook chuckled.

"That is honest at any rate. Most governesses would have claimed they were extremely proficient in everything about those three countries."

"Anyone who lies is not really suitable to teach children," answered Lolita.

She did not realise that Lord Seabrook's eyes were twinkling again as he deliberately but subtly tried to learn more about her.

'If she was really a governess,' he thought, 'she would not have been able to travel to those countries, because she must have been only a very young girl at the time.'

He looked at Lolita and thought again how lovely she was before he continued his thoughts,

'Therefore she must have gone with her parents who could afford the journey and the expenses which are always larger than one expects.'

As they turned for home, he told himself he did not know very much more about Mrs. Bell than when they had started.

'She is clever enough not to make any mistakes in what she says. At the same time she does not realise that she is speaking to me as if she was an equal, which is something no ordinary governess would do.'

Because she was not shy she talked to him as she would have talked to any other young man whom she had met in a private house.

They returned to the castle and Lord Seabrook said that he wanted Simon to have breakfast with him so that he could tell him how much he enjoyed the ride.

"We will all go to the breakfast room," he announced,"and I expect, Barty, you will have thought of it already."

"I did think your Lordship would want Master Simon with you," the butler replied tactfully.

Without thinking, Lolita had taken off her hat as they entered the hall and she put it down on a chair with her riding gloves. She had arranged her hair more tightly and neatly so that it would make her look older.

Now from the exercise there were little curls draped on her forehead and her cheeks and the sun coming through the windows shone on her hair turning it to gold.

Lord Seabrook considered that it impossible for anyone to look so beautiful and ethereal.

She might have been the Goddess Diana coming down from Olympus to associate with human beings.

Simon was chattering away about his pony.

"I would like to ride him again this afternoon please, Uncle James."

"If you want to, but you must first ask Mrs. Bell what she has planned for you. It might be time for lessons and you will have to sit at a desk."

He was teasing and Simon came back,

"Lolo'll not do anything so boring and if we are in the castle, she has hundreds of stories to tell me about the people who lived here and the battles they fought when they were so very brave."

"I am sure they were and I was wondering if perhaps instead of the castle you would like to explore my yacht."

"A ship!" Simon exclaimed. "That would be spiffing! Can it go very fast?"

"I hope you will think so, but of course not as fast as you can go on you pony."

"We can't race them as one is on the water and the other is on the ground."

"That is true," replied his uncle. "At the same time I think you would like to see the mountains at the far end of the lake and the other parts of Ullswater which are nearly as beautiful as here."

He realised as he spoke that Lolita was looking at him with wide eyes.

"That sounds wonderful, my Lord," she said, "and I know Simon will be thrilled to be on a yacht. He was looking for boats on the lake as soon as he awoke this morning."

"Well that is just what we'll do," Lord Seabrook said, "and of course I hope my other guest will join us."

He spoke as if he had only just thought of her.

Lolita hoped that Lady Cressington would refuse the invitation, but she told herself that would be asking too much.

Although she was complaining that she had always disliked yachts, Lady Cressington took an early luncheon with them and it was only reluctantly that she agreed to go aboard.

Simon was so excited at the idea that he talked endlessly to his uncle all through luncheon.

Because she was not receiving his Lordship's undivided attention, Lady Cressington was extremely cross.

Lord Seabrook obviously enjoyed answering the questions Simon asked, because they were so intelligent and he did not welcome the 'beauty's' sulky expression and the way she continually attempted to capture his attention.

She was trying to make him talk exclusively to her.

Lolita, knowing what was expected of her, did not say a word unless she was addressed.

As luncheon progressed she began to feel a little anxious. Perhaps Lady Cressington would be able to divert Lord Seabrook's interest in Simon back to herself.

They left the dining room to get ready to board the yacht.

As they did so Lolita heard Lady Cressington say,

"I always think, James, that it is a mistake for children to come down for meals when they should be in the schoolroom. It really does prevent one from having an intelligent conversation."

"I thought," replied Lord Seabrook, "that the conversation at luncheon was extremely bright for a small boy who is not yet eight years old."

"I am afraid I find children of that age extremely boring," Lady Cressington huffed, "unless of course they were my own."

As she was speaking she gave his Lordship a sideways glance, which told Lolita all too clearly that she intended to marry him.

It was something that worried her all through the afternoon although the cruise on the yacht was fascinating.

The beauty of the mountains was breath-taking and although the lake was completely calm and the yacht moved very slowly through the water, Lady Cressington clung to Lord Seabrook's arm as if she was afraid she might fall in.

She was obviously whispering intimate words in his ear which she had no wish for anyone else to hear.

Lolita kept out of the way as much as possible, but she enjoyed being on board the yacht almost as much as Simon did.

It was the very latest model and an exceptionally fine acquisition.

The Captain and the crew were delighted to welcome guests aboard and Lolita managed to see all the cabins, which were furnished most attractively and so expertly planned that she was sure that no guest would feel cramped even if they undertook a long voyage.

The Master Cabin, which of course was the largest, boasted every modern convenience it was possible to imagine.

There was a bathroom with a shower opening out of it and the curtains and covers on the bed were extremely pretty. The Saloon, which was all in green, had been, she learned, arranged and decorated entirely by its owner.

Lord Seabrook was apparently intensely interested in all the new gadgets that were now available for modern yachts.

*

They came back earlier than planned to the castle because Lady Cressington complained that she was feeling tired.

It was only then that she actually spoke to Lolita for the first time that day, having ignored her when she had first appeared in the morning. All through luncheon and while they were aboard the yacht she said nothing to her.

When they reached the castle Lord Seabrook took Simon to see a picture of his yacht which he had promised to show him.

Lady Cressington walked up the front stairs with Lolita following her and when they reached the top, her Ladyship turned round to face her.

"I find it quite unnecessary, Mrs. Bell, that you should accompany us everywhere we go. You must have enough tact to realise that his Lordship and I wish to be alone. If he wants his nephew to come with him, the child does not require a bodyguard. In future you will kindly stay in the schoolroom, where you belong."

She spoke in a hard and offensive tone of voice, very unlike the cooing seductive way she addressed Lord Seabrook.

Lolita did not answer and Lady Cressington tossed her head and walked away towards her room.

When she had gone Lolita became conscious that Mrs. Shepherd had been waiting for her in the shadows.

"Don't be upset, Mrs. Bell, at what her Ladyship says to you, as she's jealous of anyone who even speaks to his Lordship. A fine day it'll be for all of us if she gets her way."

They turned towards the stairs leading up to the schoolroom.

"I suppose," said Lolita in a small voice, "her Ladyship means to marry him."

"She'll get him by hook or by crook," muttered Mrs. Shepherd, "and a sad day it'll be for all of us, including Master Simon."

"What do you mean?"

"Mr. Barty was telling me that at dinner last night she kept saying that little boys were at their best and their happiest when they were at school. She was recommending some schools she knew where he could go before going to Eton."

Lolita became worried.

"I have always understood from my father that when a family can afford it the boys have a tutor before they go to Eton or whichever Public School is chosen for their education."

"That's what happened to his lordship and Master Simon's father," Mrs. Shepherd pointed out. "But some people who don't care much for their children send them off when they're eight and if you ask me it's far too young."

"I maintain," insisted Lolita, "and it would be a great mistake for Master Simon to go away to school until he has fully recovered from the way he has been treated by his stepmother."

"It was wicked and cruel of any woman to behave as I hear she behaved," said Mrs. Shepherd angrily. "I never did like her and it surprised me, except that he was lonely, that Mr. Rupert married again."

She sighed before she continued,

"Master Simon's mother was an angel come down from Heaven itself, and I can only imagine that woman trapped him as her Ladyship will trap his Lordship unless we can somehow prevent it."

Lolita became even more concerned about Simon as she knew that however much he was enjoying himself at the moment, the hell he had suffered must still be at the back of his mind and it would be impossible for him to adjust to a strange school at present.

"If you ask me," Mrs. Shepherd was saying, "Master Simon will find his step-aunt as bad as his stepmother."

"Why do you say that?"

"Because of the way she treats the staff," replied Mrs. Shepherd.

They had reached the schoolroom by this time and she sat down in the armchair by the fireplace as if she was breathless before resuming,

"She's so disagreeable to her lady's maid that I wonder the woman stays, and if Master Simon's stepmother beat him that's just what her Ladyship will do when he's in her power."

"Then we must somehow stop it," cried Lolita. "We cannot allow this to happen again. It would be too cruel and wicked."

She was thinking as she spoke that she would take Simon away if there was the slightest chance of it happening, but she had no idea where she would go or how she could pay, but somehow she must save him.

"Now don't you fret yourself," Mrs. Shepherd was saying. "It hasn't happened yet and with any luck his Lordship will see sense afore he goes too far. But make no mistake that woman's after him and if she gets what she wants it'll be goodbye for most of us and Heaven knows what'll happen to that poor little boy."

She looked at the clock and gave an exclamation.

"I must go and see what's happening downstairs. You can never trust these young housemaids! However much you tell them, it goes in one ear and out the other."

She was still talking as she left the room.

Lolita sat down on a chair.

How could it be possible that Simon could have walked from one hell into what might become another?

'I must save him,' she thought. 'Oh please, God, he cannot suffer all that again!'

Then just as if it was an answer to her prayer she felt something come into her memory.

Something she had entirely forgotten, which had happened about three months ago.

It was almost as if the clouds which had encompassed the mountains at the end of the lake were moving slowly away and as they cleared she could feel her memory coming back to her.

It was something which she had heard, but which she had forgotten until this very moment.

CHAPTER FIVE

Lolita recalled that she had been attending a luncheon party in London and when the meal was over a number of the young people present moved into the garden.

She had stayed behind for a moment talking to the hostess about her mother as they had been great friends.

Then the door had opened and the hostess's eldest son came in.

"Hallo, Harry!" she exclaimed. "I did not expect you until later."

"I got away early," he replied.

"Have you had luncheon?" his mother asked.

"Yes, I have, thank you, but I have told a servant to bring me a drink. I need one as I am in such a rage."

"A rage! What has happened?"

"You will hardly believe it," he continued, "and I myself find it very difficult to comprehend."

"Tell me," his mother implored.

The young man sat down in the nearest chair.

"You know Captain Michael Duncan, who is in the Regiment with me."

"Yes of course. Such a nice young gentleman! I am always glad to see him."

"I did not tell you," Harry went on, "that he became secretly engaged to Catherine Cressington."

"The great beauty?"

"Yes, and she has been dangling him about for some time in a way which I thought was most unkind."

Lolita noticed that her hostess pursed her lips together and it was obvious that she disapproved of Catherine Cressington.

"Because they are engaged," Harry resumed, "and she is very fond of jewellery, Michael lent her a magnificent necklace which his father had brought back from India. The General was very proud of it."

"Why particularly?"

"Because he had received it as a gift from a Maharajah whose life he had saved and it is absolutely fantastic.

"I think I have heard people talking about it," replied his mother.

"I am not surprised. It is an arrangement of enormous emeralds, rubies, sapphires and of course diamonds. It is worth a fortune."

"And I suppose it will be Michael's one day."

"It would have been, except that it has disappeared from around the neck of Catherine Cressington!"

His mother stared at him.

"What do you mean?"

"I mean what I say," answered Harry. "Michael lent it to her to wear for one particular party she was attending. Then on their way home she told him she no longer wished to marry him and that, as you can imagine, upset him very much."

"Of course it did and I am very sorry for Michael. I can only hope it does not break his heart. "What has broken his heart," added Harry, "is that Catherine Cressington has disappeared and so has the necklace."

"Do you mean she has taken it with her?"

"She has stolen it if you want the truth," asserted Harry. "The General is furious and there is nothing poor Michael can do as she cannot be found."

"But she is such a success," exclaimed his mother. "Everyone in London is talking about her beauty."

"I know that, but Michael thinks she now has some other man she wants to marry who has a title. Apparently she always resented the fact that he would have to wait a long time to inherit his father's title as the General is in very good health."

"I have never heard of anything so disgraceful," his mother declared. "But surely eventually she will send him back the necklace."

"I very much doubt it, but if you ask me she is hoping to keep it when all the fuss and commotion has died down."

"Well, I call it stealing," his mother fumed. "There is no other word for it."

Lolita could now remember thinking that Lady Cressington, whom she had seen once at a large party, must be a very strange woman.

She could not imagine her mother or indeed any of her friends stealing anything, even if it was something quite inexpensive, but to go off with a trophy such as Harry had described was shocking, to say the very least of it.

She knew well how magnificent Indian jewels could be and although she had never been to India, her father had a friend who used to call occasionally at their little house in the country. He was a great traveller and on one occasion he had come back from India with a present for her mother.

It was a brooch of typically Indian workmanship set with small precious stones and it was very pretty. There were earrings and a ring to match it.

Lolita's mother had been delighted with the gift and her father's friend had told them about some of the magnificent jewels he had seen in the Palaces of the Maharajahs.

"They are worth a King's ransom," he had claimed, "and are passed down from generation to generation. They would no more think of selling them than of changing their names."

However, a year later when they were very hard-up, someone offered her mother quite a considerable sum and she had been forced to sell them.

Lolita had not thought again about the Indian jewels until this moment.

Now this conversation came back clearly to her and she also remembered that she had told a friend what she had heard and he had told her,

"I know Michael Duncan. He is a very nice young man and the General is the best Commander the Brigade of has ever had. When I next see him in White's, I will tell him how sorry I am to hear about his loss."

Knowing how badly Lady Cressington had behaved, Lolita knew what she must now do, and she could understood why she had disappeared from London where she was being such a success and why she had come North to hide in Lord Seabrook's castle.

The necklace was of course not the main reason for her departure as having met Lord Seabrook she was determined to marry him.

It would certainly be a very much better marriage than to a Captain in the Brigade of Guards – even if his father was a General and a Baronet.

'I must now save Lord Seabrook as well as Simon,' Lolita told herself.

She wondered how she should go about it and when she thought the whole situation over in her mind, she realised she had two important facts on her side.

Firstly that Captain Michael Duncan was looking for Lady Cressington, but could not find her and secondly that he was a member of White's Club in St. James's.

She had heard her father talking about his beloved White's so often and whatever else he gave up he had no intention of ceasing to be a member.

She went to her bedroom and taking a sheet of writing-paper wrote on it,

"*The necklace you seek is at Castle Seabrook, Ullswater.*"

She hesitated for a moment and then wrote at the bottom,

"*A Friend.*"

She addressed it to Captain Michael Duncan at White's Club and walked downstairs to the hall.

She had noticed yesterday that the post arrived twice a day – once in the morning and once in the afternoon. His Lordship's secretary usually had a lot of letters waiting for the postman and he would place them on a tray which lay on a table under the stairs.

Lolita hoped there would be some letters there now and was not disappointed. There was in fact quite a pile of envelopes already stamped and she knew they would be collected by the postman when he delivered the letters in about an hour's time.

She slipped her letter addressed to the Captain under the others and quickly returned upstairs again to the schoolroom.

She reckoned it would be several days, not less than three or four, before there was a response of any sort.

*

The following morning she rode again with Lord Seabrook and Simon was, for the first time, allowed off a leading-rein.

"Now I am really riding like Papa," he hooted excitedly.

"Then you must be as good as he was," said Lolita.

"I am good now, am I not, Uncle James?" asked Simon.

"Very good indeed," his uncle told him, "but you have got to be better still if you are to keep up with Lolo."

Simon chuckled.

"When I have a horse as big as hers, I will race her."

"And I will race you too," said Lord Seabrook, "so you must be able to beat us both."

Lolita smiled at him, thinking how sensible he was with Simon.

If the terrible Lady Cressington was not at the castle, she believed that Simon would at last have a home where he need not be afraid.

She now knew how disagreeable her Ladyship could be and she now found it all the more unpleasant to sit at the luncheon table and watch her flirting with Lord Seabrook, insinuating in every way she could that she wanted to be alone with him.

Lady Cressington was determined that Simon and his governess should take luncheon in the schoolroom and she was very angry when she learned from her lady's maid that Lolita had been out riding with Lord Seabrook before breakfast every morning.

She had not been aware of it at first, but on the fourth day after they had come to the castle she said to Lolita after Lord Seabrook had left the room,

"I understand, Mrs. Bell, you have been out riding every morning and as I believe Simon is accompanied by a groom, there is no reason for you to ride too. In future you will stay in the castle and wait for the boy's return."

"Is this an order from his Lordship?" asked Lolita innocently.

"It is an order from me," asserted Lady Cressington.

"You obviously do not know your place as a governess, which I can quite understand as you are far too young to be one. Therefore you are taking liberties which you have no right to."

She almost spat the words at Lolita, who thought it would be a mistake to reply and so she walked out of the room without saying anything.

She was well aware, however, that Lady Cressington was glaring at her back with a furious expression on her face.

Lolita was quite certain she would try to make Lord Seabrook dismiss her.

'If I have to leave,' she thought, 'I will take Simon with me and we will hide somewhere where no one will find us.'

At the same time she was well aware that the money she had taken with her would not last for ever.

Lord Seabrook had been kind enough to instruct his secretary to pay her back everything she had spent in bringing Simon to the castle. She had made a list of everything the journey had cost, writing down what she had paid for post-chaises and what she had spent at the inns on the way.

She had then given the list to Simon.

"I want you to add this up for me," she suggested, "and then take it to his Lordship's secretary. You must count what he gives you to be certain he is right and that he pays you what you have added up."

Simon stared at the list and very slowly with a little help from Lolita he added it all up.

After two or three attempts he got it right and she said,

"Thank you so much. It is something I hate doing myself, it really is a man's job."

"Shall I take it downstairs now?"

"Yes, of course, and if you see your uncle, show him how clever you have been in getting the sum right."

Simon went away and when he came back he said,

"Uncle James said it was very clever of me and he gave me ten shillings all to myself!"

He showed Lolita the coins.

"Now I can buy you a present. What do you want very, very much?"

Lolita knew he would be disappointed if she said she wanted nothing and so they went to the village at the top of the lake and she chose an inexpensive but pretty ornament made to represent the castle.

Simon was delighted with it too.

"Now when you look at it you will always think of the castle," he told her.

"Of course I will, but it is more fun looking at the castle in real life!"

"That is what I think," agreed Simon. "Now we can go home and climb right up to the top of the tower again."

It amused him to be able to look out from such a height.

Lolita told him stories of how his ancestors had stationed sentries on the tower where they watched for any enemy who might approach them.

Later that day Lord Seabrook asked to see Lolita.

"I think it was very kind of you to spend so much money bringing Simon to me. He showed me what it had cost you."

"It was actually a lesson in arithmetic, my Lord," replied Lolita. "He added up the list with a little difficulty and because I told him to do so, he checked everything your secretary gave him."

Lord Seabrook laughed.

"I cannot understand, how you can be so astute with children. You are little more than one yourself."

"Perhaps I think the same way as they do – and want the same things."

"What do you want?" he enquired.

"I suppose the answer to that question is happiness, and Simon and I are very happy here with you, my Lord."

She almost added 'except for one thing,' but that would have been impertinent.

"I am glad to hear it and that you are giving Simon some basic lessons, even if they are rather unusual ones!"

"They will become more serious in time," said Lolita, "but he has already learnt almost enough history to write a book himself, and I want, with your permission, to take him to see Walcott Priory so that I can tell him about the monastic orders who came to England and what they achieved in many parts of the country, including Norfolk and Canterbury and,although I was not aware of it, in Ullswater too."

"You are obviously very well educated, Mrs. Bell."

"I have loved reading just as I have loved riding."

"And you also love children," remarked Lord Seabrook. "What about men?"

He saw to his surprise a strange look come into her eyes.

Then she said quickly,

"I must go and find Simon. He is in the garden with the dog you have given him and he is not yet quite certain how to control it."

She had gone before Lord Seabrook could think of an excuse to keep her talking to him.

He felt that she now puzzled him even more that she had done previously.

*

Later the next afternoon Lady Cressington insisted that Lord Seabrook should take her for a drive.

Lolita went down to the library to try and find a book she wanted and discovered to her delight that the library was up-to-date.

There were not only a number of books she wanted to read herself, but many with illustrations which were exactly what she required for Simon and she picked up three books which she knew he would find interesting.

She had left him in the schoolroom writing a list of dog's names as he had not yet named his dog, as she thought it was good for his hand-writing as well as using his brain to think up suitable names.

She was passing the study door which was wide open and as she did so, she saw, as she had noticed earlier, the newspapers placed on a stool in front of the fireplace.

She had not read a newspaper since she had come to the castle. There did not seem to be time and no one thought to bring one up to the schoolroom.

She walked into the study and picked up *The Morning Post*.

She opened it, wondering what was happening in the big world beyond Ullswater. She read the headlines one by one and found there seemed to be nothing very startling.

Then as she turned another page she saw the Court Circular and beside it the obituary column.

It was headed,

"Mrs. Ralph Piran."

Lolita felt as if her heart stood still as she read on,

"Mrs. Ralph Piran, formerly the Countess of Walcott, died yesterday at 26 Park Lane. She had been unwell for several months."

The obituary went on to give the date she had married the Earl of Walcott and it reported that they had left their ancestral home on Ullswater to live quietly in Worcestershire.

It mentioned at the end that there was one daughter of her first marriage, Lady Lolita Vernon. She was abroad, but had been informed of her mother's death.

Lolita read the article through twice.

Then putting down the newspaper she ran upstairs to the schoolroom and by the time she reached it the tears were running down her cheeks.

Although she tried to wipe them away, Simon looked up when she appeared.

"You are crying, Lolo," he exclaimed. "What has hurt you?"

Lolita collapsed into an armchair and Simon rushed to put his arms around her neck.

"Don't cry, Lolo," he pleaded. "Who has been unkind to you?"

"I have just – learned," spluttered Lolita, "that my mother has – gone to – God. She was very ill, so I could not say – goodbye to her – but I shall miss her *so* very much."

"My Mama and Papa are with God," said Simon gently, "you told me so."

"Yes, of course they are and we can – talk to them in – our prayers."

"I cried when my mother died," said Simon, "but now I love you and I would cry and cry if you died."

"I am not going to die, Simon, and I believe your mother sent me to you so that I can look after you."

"That was very clever of her. If you had not found me, Step-mama might have caught up with me and taken me back."

His arm tightened instinctively as he added,

"Then she would have beaten me again because I had dared to run away."

"It is something you are not to think about," Lolita told him, "because you are very happy here."

"You must be happy too, otherwise I shall cry like you are."

"I don't want you to cry," said Lolita, hugging him.

At the same time because he was so loving the tears kept running down her cheeks.

Simon kissed her.

"You are not to cry," he insisted. "How can I make you happy?"

"You make me happy because you love me and so I will try not to cry any more."

She held him close for a moment and then went to her bedroom to wash her face.

It had been such a shock to know her mother was dead and that she would never see her again. She wondered vaguely if her stepfather would marry someone else and she was sure that with all his money he would find quite a number of women very willing to do so.

Equally she could not help being afraid as if he felt lonely he might want her back not only to keep him company, but to make it possible for him to attend the social events he would not otherwise have been invited to.

'I will never go back now,' she decided with determination.

Lolita had felt that even though her mother was unconscious, she afforded her some measure of protection, but now she was gone she would be completely at the mercy of her stepfather and undoubtedly Murdock Tanner as well.

She walked back into the schoolroom, picked up the books she had brought from the library and started to show Simon the pictures.

They were sitting in one armchair close together when Lord Seabrook entered the room.

"I wondered where you were," he said, "and as Lady Cressington has a headache and has gone to lie down, I thought you would like to come down and join me for tea."

Simon jumped up out of the chair.

"We would love to, Uncle James, but you must be very kind to Lolo because she's unhappy."

"Unhappy! Why? What has happened."

He looked towards Lolita as he spoke and she felt he must notice that her eyes were swollen.

"It is – nothing – important," she began to say, but Simon interrupted her.

"Lolo's mother is dead, Uncle James, and she is missing her, just like I missed Mama when she died and they took her away in a black box."

"I am very sorry to hear this news," Lord Seabrook said to Lolita. "It must be a great shock. I had actually thought that as you never mentioned your parents you are an orphan."

"My mother was very ill and not able to recognise anyone when I left London," replied Lolita in a low voice. "She was being well looked after, otherwise I could not have brought Simon to you."

"Come down and give me my tea and tell me more about your family," suggested Lord Seabrook. "What other relations do have you?"

Lolita rose from the chair.

"I have none, my Lord," she said firmly, "absolutely none and I do not want to talk about it."

There was nothing more he could say, but he was even more curious.

Despite the orders Lady Cressington had given Lolita, she was riding with Lord Seabrook again before breakfast the next morning.

And to please Simon they had been sailing on the lake in a small boat with a red sail and he was even more thrilled with it than he had been with the yacht.

Because he looked so happy, Lolita felt happy too.

She had cried herself to sleep when she went to bed.

Although her mother had been in a coma long before she left London, there was always the hope that she would get better and she enjoyed the feeling that she herself belonged to someone.

Now she was entirely on her own and when she thought of the future she became frightened.

She wanted to claim her mother's belongings and also any money and jewellery which she might have left her. And yet if she did so she would have to be in touch with her stepfather and that was something she dared not do.

It was frightening to think that her only possessions in whole world were her clothes, her mother's ring and the two hundred pounds she had taken from her stepfather's safe.

She hoped and prayed that she would be able to stay on at the castle, but Simon would eventually go to school and what would happen to her then?

But what was more likely was that if Lady Cressington got her way she would be turned out in a week or so.

Then she would have to make a terrible decision.

Whether to take Simon with her and disappear or leave him to suffer once again as he had suffered before.

It all churned over and over in her mind.

She found it difficult to sleep because she could not answer the questions, which kept occurring and re-occurring.

However, when they came back to the castle from their sail they were all laughing and as there was no sign of Lady Cressington, they went happily into the dining room.

They had only just sat down when she joined them and Lord Seabrook rose as she entered the room.

She was looking rather overdressed and wearing too much jewellery for the country.

"Had you forgotten about me?" she simpered.

"I thought you would be having luncheon upstairs,"replied Lord Seabrook a little lamely.

From the way he spoke Lolita guessed he had actually forgotten that Lady Cressington was in the castle and had been thinking instead of Simon and his delight at sailing in the little boat.

Lady Cressington sat down and Barty quickly poured some wine into her glass.

"I heard you were sailing on the lake," she said, "so I did not hurry, but I am sure you and I could find something more exciting to do this afternoon."

She flickered her eyelashes at Lord Seabrook as she spoke and then became aware that he was looking at Simon.

"How is your dear little nephew getting on with his lessons?" she asked. "It seems to me he does not spend much time in the schoolroom. You must not allow him to grow up to be an ignoramus."

"I am extremely impressed with what he has learned already," responded Lord Seabrook, "which is a great deal of history and some arithmetic which I am sure I could not have achieved at his age."

"Oh, I am sure you could have done," purred Lady Cressington. "You are so intelligent now that you must have been very clever when you were a little boy."

She put her hand on Lord Seabrook's and although it was obvious he was expected to raise it to his lips, he did not do so.

Almost as if Simon thought Lady Cressington was attacking Lolita, he piped up,

"Lolo teaches me very well. She says I am going to be very clever like Papa and Uncle James."

"But of course you will," said Lady Cressington smoothly. "But what you need is a tutor, which I am quite certain your kind uncle can find for you and he will teach you the subjects you must know about when you go to school and later to Oxford."

Simon frowned.

"I don't want a tutor. I want Lolo. She teaches me very exciting things. I know lots and lots of history."

There was a defiant note in his voice.

Lady Cressington gave a silvery little laugh.

"That is very loyal of you, but in a little while you will learn that Lolo, as you call her, is too young to know all the lessons a big boy like you has to learn."

Simon was obviously about to make an angry retort, but Lolita put out her hand and laid it on his arm.

"I want *you*," stressed Simon firmly.

Then before anyone else could speak, Barty appeared at the door to announce,

"Captain Michael Duncan to see you, my Lord."

Lord Seabrook looked up in astonishment.

Lolita felt her heart leap as a tall, good-looking young man came into the dining room.

He walked towards Lord Seabrook, who rose and held out his hand.

"This is indeed a surprise, Michael. I had no idea you were in this neighbourhood."

"Although I am delighted to see you, James," replied Captain Duncan, "I have come on a very different errand."

"What is that?" asked Lord Seabrook.

The Captain looked at Lady Cressington. "

I have come to ask you for the return of the necklace which belongs to my father and which you did not return to me when you left London."

"You gave it to me," said Lady Cressington imperiously.

"That is untrue!" retorted Captain Duncan. "We were, as everybody now knows, secretly engaged, and I lent it to you because you wanted to wear it at the Duchess's ball. When I asked for it back, you told me you had no further use for me, but you did not return the necklace."

Lord Seabrook looked in bewilderment from one to the other.

"What is all this about?" he demanded.

"I apologise, James, for making a scene in your castle, but I expect you will have heard, as most people have, of the magnificent necklace which was given to my father after he saved the life of the Maharajah of Jovnelos. He wanted it to be handed down as a family heirloom, but to put it bluntly her Ladyship here has absconded with it!"

"That is untrue, quite untrue!" snapped Lady Cressington, her voice rising sharply. "You gave it to me as a present and as a present I accepted it."

"That is a lie," countered Captain Duncan, "and my father has already informed the Police that his property has been stolen."

Lady Cressington went very pale and for a moment there was silence.

Then Lord Seabrook turned to his butler.

"Barty, will you send a footman up to her Ladyship's bedroom to bring down her jewel case and pour Captain Duncan a glass of wine."

"It is something I need," said the Captain gratefully. "My father has given me hell for parting with the necklace in the first place, and I am deeply hurt and distressed that any woman to whom I offered my name and my heart should behave in such a monstrous way!"

He spoke harshly – almost as if he was on the parade ground.

Lady Cressington stared at him in a fury and would have risen to her feet, but Lord Seabrook, however, put out his hand to prevent her from rising.

"No, wait!" he said sharply. "Until the necklace has been handed over."

Then turning to his new visitor he asked in a conversational tone,

"How did you get here, Michael?"

"I was informed where the necklace was to be found by a kind friend whom I imagine is here in your castle. took the first train available to Penrith and came on at speed in a post-chaise."

"Someone in the castle told you where the necklace was," Lord Seabrook said slowly, almost to himself.

"I am exceedingly grateful that I have such a friend. It has saved me from a great deal of trouble with my father and has prevented, I hope, a scandal which would undoubtedly be published in the newspapers if it was known that such a famous necklace had been taken from us in such an extraordinary manner."

Lady Cressington turned towards Lord Seabrook pleadingly.

"You must believe me, James. He gave it to me and it is mine."

"I believe it is usual when an engagement is terminated," replied Lord Seabrook quietly, "that all presents the bride-to-be has received and generally all letters are returned to the giver."

Lady Cressington could find nothing more to say.

At that moment a footman appeared carrying a large leather case engraved with Lady Cressington's initials surmounted by a coronet.

He would have taken it to Lady Cressington, but Captain Duncan took it from him before he could reach her.

Putting the case down on the floor beside Lord Seabrook's chair he opened it to reveal a number of jewels all in their compartments. He pushed the smaller ones aside to bring up a large box from the very bottom. It was of crimson velvet and embroidered in an Eastern fashion which was immediately recognisable.

The Captain took it out and putting it on the table beside Lord Seabrook, he opened it.

113

As he did so Simon gave a loud gasp of astonishment and Lolita felt like doing the same.

The necklace lying on white velvet was even more remarkable than anyone could have expected.

To begin with it was very large and made in the shape of a heart with a huge diamond in the centre, surmounted by rubies and emeralds, all very large in size, while the heart itself was edged with pearls.

Smaller diamonds glittered between the larger stones and the neck-chain was of emeralds, graduated from small to those which were as large as a shilling when they reached the heart-shaped pendant.

It was not surprising, Lolita thought, that the General did not want to lose anything so unique. She seemed to remember reading that the Maharajah in question owned his own mines and she was sure that the necklace would have been made by his own people. It might have taken years to create such perfection both in workmanship and in the stones themselves.

"You can understand," said the Captain quietly, "why my father has no wish to lose this valuable heirloom and I can only thank you, James, for returning it to me."

"I am sure," commented Lord Seabrook," it was what Lady Cressington intended to do. She is in fact leaving us this afternoon. I am sending her to Carlisle, where she will catch the evening express to London. It may have been a bother for you, Michael, to make the journey, but I am delighted to see you and I hope you will stay with us tonight at any rate."

"I shall be delighted to do so," accepted the Captain.

Lady Cressington rose to her feet.

She was pale but her eyes were dark with anger.

She realised that she had lost the man she intended to marry, had been dismissed ignominiously and there was nothing she could say about it.

She therefore swept from the room without a backward glance at anyone.

Barty, without being told, closed her jewel case, picked it up and he too left the dining room.

When he had gone a footman hurried to fill the Captain's glass.

For a moment there was an almost uncomfortable silence until Simon broke it. He jumped up from his chair and ran to his uncle's side.

"I want to see the big necklace again," he said. "It shines as if it has little lights inside it."

This was because the sun had just reached the dining room table.

Lord Seabrook laughed.

"At least you have found what you were seeking,Michael, and I do not blame your father for wishing to keep such a fabulous piece in the family."

"He is determined that it will be passed down from generation to generation," he replied. "And as we own nothing else anything as valuable, he hopes that when he has gone there will be something he will be remembered for."

He paused and then added,

"You can say the same of your castle, James."

"Now you are being morbid. I have no intention of dying yet. I have a great many things to do before I leave this world."

"I feel the same," said the Captain. "But I can promise you one thing, James. I have no intention of marrying for a very long time. As my nanny used to say to me, 'once bitten, twice shy'."

Lord Seabrook laughed and Simon was interested.

"What did bite you?" he asked the Captain.

"Something very sneaky and unpleasant," he answered, "and I hope it will never happen to you."

"Did it hurt you?"

"Yes, it hurt me, but I am not going to be hurt another time."

"Step-mama beat me and it hurt very, very much," Simon told him. "I screamed and cried, but she would not stop."

The Captain looked at Lord Seabrook in astonishment.

"What is all this?"

"It is something I want Simon to forget."

Lord Seabrook put his arm round Simon and held him close.

"Now you are happy here," he said, "and Lolo is looking after you, I want you to promise me that you will never mention your stepmother again. Forget her just as the Captain is going to forget that someone took away his beautiful necklace. Now it is his again and he is going to keep it safe for ever."

With an intelligence Lolita thought commendable,

Simon put his head on one side and asked,

"Am I safe for ever?"

"Absolutely and completely safe and I promise you that is the truth."

Simon gave a little sound and put his cheek against his uncle's arm.

"I like being here with you, Uncle James. It's very, very exciting and no one can ever take me away."

"No one shall ever take you away," repeated Lord Seabrook firmly.

Simon moved away to go back to Lolita.

"Let us go and find Bracken," he said.

He had finally decided that Bracken was to be the name of his dog, as Lolita had told him that there would be bracken on the hills in the autumn and his dog would then want to go shooting with his uncle and pick up the game.

Bracken was not allowed into the dining room until he had received a little more training, but he was waiting outside in the hall with a footman.

He ran eagerly towards Simon as soon as he appeared and Simon put his arms round him going down onto one knee.

"He's been very good, Master Simon," the footman said. "If you go on teaching him to obey you, you'll find he'll be as good as any of his Lordship's dogs."

"That is just what I want him to be."

Simon went to the front door taking Bracken with him and they ran on the grass to the other side of the courtyard.

Lolita stood on the steps in the sunshine and sent up a prayer of thankfulness to God.

She had got rid of Lady Cressington and now she could remain at the castle without being afraid of Simon being sent away to school.

She could hardly believe that her letter had achieved exactly as she had planned nor that Captain Duncan would arrive so quickly.

Now that she had seen the necklace she could understand how much it meant to him and his father.

She thought to herself that this was another jump she had taken and high and difficult though it had been, she had landed safely.

She could only thank God, who she was sure had helped her and because her mother, wherever she might be,would have understood her predicament, had helped her too.

'Thank you, thank you,' she muttered.

She felt the sunshine enveloping her as if with a kiss of love.

CHAPTER SIX

Lolita was too tactful to go down to dinner that night as she felt it would be uncomfortable after the day's drama.

Her great relief was that Lady Cressington had departed and therefore Simon was no longer in danger.

She kept him happy in the afternoon with stories about the history of the castle and when they went into the garden there was no sign of Lord Seabrook or Captain Duncan.

Lolita wondered as she retired to bed whether on the next morning she would be able to ride with Lord Seabrook again as she had become accustomed to.

However when she was called, the maid, after drawing back the curtains said,

"His Lordship's left, ma'am, so there be no need for you to hurry. He's taken his friend the Captain to Penrith and I hears from Mr. Barty that he'll be staying a night or two with some friends."

Lolita was surprised.

She could well understand why Lord Seabrook would want to stay away from the castle for a while.

Yet she could not help a feeling of depression – or was it loss – that she would not see him either today or tomorrow.

Then she told herself that she was being very stupid.

Of course Lord Seabrook would feel embarrassed after he had learned of Lady Cressington's extraordinary behaviour and he would want to be with friends and forget the whole unfortunate saga.

This explanation, she concluded, was more than likely.

But Lolita had no idea that his Lordship had another and very different reason for leaving the castle.

He had lain awake last night thinking how glad he was not to have Lady Cressington clinging to him any more.

At the same time he was acutely aware of his feelings for Lolita and he could not explain them to himself.

But he found it almost impossible not to think of her every moment of the day.

It was not only because she was so incredibly lovely that he wanted to gaze at her beautiful features.

She affected him in a way that was deeper and different from anything he had ever felt for any other woman.

'It is madness to think of her in this way,' he thought angrily as he dressed for dinner.

How was it possible he kept asking himself that he could feel like this for an employee?

She was his nephew's governess and he knew nothing about her, except that she was too young and too pretty to be teaching anyone.

Lady Cressington had indeed made that point very clear to him and he had refused to listen when she had urged him to send Lolita away.

Now he found it impossible to stop dreaming about Mrs. Bell when she was not in the same room and he was forced to concede that he found himself absurdly content whenever she was present.

He decided that everything had grown out of focus and therefore he had left the castle for a day or so to try and put his life back into its right perspective.

He had some good friends who lived close to Penrith, Norman and Bridget Harrison, who had begged him over and over again to stay with them at their lovely house at Inglewood, when he needed to visit the town.

He felt that this was a good moment to accept their invitation and so he instructed his valet to pack his bag and to come with him.

He told Barty to look after the castle and Master Simon.

He drove away, handling with his usual expertise a fine team of horses he was very proud of.

Yet he could not help regretting that he was not waiting at the stables for Mrs. Bell and Simon to join him.

*

Because they were on their own, Simon was thrilled to be free to explore more of the castle and he wanted to spend as much time as possible down by the lake.

Lolita considered it was a good opportunity to teach him to swim. She had been surprised that he had not learnt sooner until she heard that there was no river or pool near the house where he had lived in the country.

"All boys should be able to swim," she told Simon, "and now I will give you your first lesson if Mrs. Shepherd can provide us with suitable clothes for bathing."

Of course Mrs. Shepherd had found exactly what they required in her Aladdin's cave in the attic.

The bathing-dress for Lolita was slightly old-fashioned, but it fitted her and was, she thought, particularly becoming.

She found herself wishing that Lord Seabrook could see her in it and then she blushed and rebuked herself for wishing anything so improper.

Simon learned to swim extremely quickly, she thought, even for a bright boy.

They swam again the next day and once more after riding on the day that Lord Seabrook was expected to return.

"I want to show Uncle James how well I can now swim," Simon said over and over again. "I'm sure he'll think it very, very clever of me to have learned so quickly."

"Of course he will," Lolita encouraged him. "You must also show him how obedient Bracken is, and how he comes to you at once when you call him."

Barty was uncertain whether his Lordship would arrive in time for luncheon, but it was not yet noon when, crossing the garden after they had been swimming, Lolita and Simon spied the horses coming up the drive.

Simon gave a hoot of joy and ran to the front of the house.

Lolita moved after him more slowly and already she could hear Simon telling his uncle how he could now swim – how obedient Bracken was and how he could now ride so fast on his pony that the groom had difficulty in keeping up with him.

It all bubbled out of his mouth from sheer excitement.

Lord Seabrook was smiling as he walked towards Lolita.

"I gather, Mrs. Bell, that you have been very busy since I left."

"Simon can swim really quite well, my Lord," she informed him. "He has taken to it like 'a duck to water'."

Lord Seabrook laughed, looking straight at Lolita with his piercing blue eyes.

"Of course, and I suppose you can swim like a mermaid."

"I would hope so," replied Lolita demurely.

Simon was so excited by his uncle's return, while Lolita was finding it impossible to suppress a strange feeling within herself. It seemed to move up through her body and into her breasts.

He was back and looking more handsome than when he had left.

"I haven't swum for years," he said as they walked into the castle, "but I am quite prepared to race you both if that is what you would like."

"I expect you will win," said Simon.

"I shall be very annoyed if I cannot beat you both, but actually I have another idea for us this afternoon."

"What is that?" asked Simon cautiously.

"I remember that Mrs. Bell wanted you to see Walcott Priory and I thought we might go there unless you have already done so whilst I have been away."

He looked at Lolita as he spoke and she answered,

"I did think about it, my Lord, and then as I understand there is a caretaker in residence, I thought he might not let us in without your assistance."

"Then I will assist you by taking you there myself this afternoon. It is a long time since I visited the Priory and I would like to see it again."

"Lolo will tell me lots and lots of stories about Walcott Priory," said Simon with satisfaction. "I would really like that."

They enjoyed a delicious luncheon and it seemed to Lolita very different from the meals they had been served for the last two days, especially with Lord Seabrook now present again.

He told Simon several stories which made him laugh, but Lolita had the strange feeling they were really meant for her.

As soon as luncheon was over another chaise was brought to the door. This was drawn by a pair of perfectly matched stallions which Lord Seabrook told Simon he had owned for nearly three years.

They were still, in his opinion, the best in his stables.

"I want to drive a chaise please, Uncle James," pleaded Simon.

"I will teach you how, as soon as you are proficient enough on your pony to jump a hedge without falling off."

"I will soon be jumping. I am riding so quickly now that Tom the groom keeps asking me to go slower because his horse cannot keep up with me!"

Lord Seabrook smiled.

"I can see we will have to give Tom a faster horse to accompany you. I know your father would be very pleased that you can ride so well."

"Lolo is very pleased with me," added Simon. "She told me this morning that when I am a little older I will ride as well as you do."

Lord Seabrook looked at Lolita.

"That is a somewhat twisted compliment, but still I accept it with pleasure."

There was something in the tone of his voice that made Lolita blush, but she could not imagine why.

She knew that it was very delightful that Lord Seabrook was back at the castle.

It was as if the sun had come out the moment he appeared.

Now as they drove towards the Priory she was thinking what fun it was now there was no Lady Cressington finding fault and disparaging her and no Captain Duncan to divert Lord Seabrook's attention from Simon and of course herself.

When Walcott Priory loomed up in front of them it was much larger than she had expected and it was also extremely beautiful.

Lord Seabrook told her that the present owner had spent a great deal of money on it and she appreciated that it would not have looked the same in her father and mother's time.

However, when they entered through the front door, Lolita felt a thrill of excitement.

She was seeing where her father had lived since he was born and where her mother had lived with him when they had first married.

The caretaker, as Lolita expected was only too pleased to allow Lord Seabrook into the Priory and invited them to look round without his assistance.

"I know I can trust you, my Lord," he said, "but I wouldn't trust most of those who comes here out of curiosity. But my leg's paining me and I've no wish to walk more than I has to."

"You can trust us," Lord Seabrook assured him, "not to touch anything and to close all the doors behind us."

They set off alone on what Lolita felt was an exciting voyage of discovery.

Her father and mother had talked so much about the Priory and how it had meant everything to them when they were first married.

She could understand how it had almost broken her father's heart to have to leave it when they had moved to London.

She had always wondered why her father had gone so far away from his home and now when she saw the Priory she realised it would have been agony for him to have lived nearby and not own it.

What she had not expected was that he would have left behind so many of the family treasures, especially the portraits of her family's ancestors.

Then she remembered that her father had said the man who had bought the Priory had insisted on purchasing it 'lock, stock and barrel', as he put it.

"As no one else wished to pay such a large sum for an enormous house," he added, "I had to accept his offer because I needed the money so desperately."

It had enabled him to pay off all his father's debts and as well he had been able to pension off the old servants who had served the family for many years.

There was just enough money left to buy the house in London where Lolita had been brought up. It had been small but comfortable and being Elizabethan held a beauty all of its own.

At the same time it was impossible to compare it with the Priory.

Lolita had learned that over one hundred monks had lived here and now she could see the size of the building she realised there was room for more.

They entered the huge hall at the front where the monks dined and where any travellers were entitled to join them.

It was just as it had always been since the time the Priory had been built. The walls were covered with oak panelling and the long refectory tables and the great medieval fireplace were untouched by the passing centuries.

Lord Seabrook had visited the Priory before and he led them next to what had been, Lolita believed, her grandmother's drawing room.

It was a lovely room with its diamond-paned bow windows looking over the garden and here, as in a number of other rooms, the mantelpieces had been added much later. Many were carved with skill and imagination by the Italian sculptors who had come to England to enhance the houses of the aristocracy.

It was, however, the pictures which Lolita liked the most. Each one gave her a pang of pain because they were no longer in the possession of her family.

There were portraits of the Earls of Walcott and of their wives and children all down the centuries. Every great artist in turn had apparently painted them.

It was miserable for Lolita to think that they would pass on to another rich man with whom they had no connection and he would doubtless not appreciate them or love them as the Walcotts had done.

She had no idea that Lord Seabrook was watching her intently as she moved from picture to picture.

He was thinking that the rapt expression on her face was something he would not have expected from any woman – let alone from someone as young as Mrs. Bell.

He led her up the wide oak carved staircase to the first floor and here they found the State bedrooms.

The huge four-poster beds had been added by every succeeding Earl and some of the most elaborate and unusual ones had actually been brought from France during and after the French Revolution.

Lolita remembered the story of how much furniture had been bought for practically nothing from the revolutionaries by the Prince of Wales, who later became George IV. He had been obliged to send his chef to buy what he wanted, because he was the only member of his staff who spoke French.

She would have liked to know if her ancestor had gone himself or merely sent an agent to act for him. Whoever it had been, his taste had been impeccable.

There was, however, no one to answer the questions she was burning to have answered.

Lolita now wished that she had asked her mother more about Walcott Priory after her father had died.

'If only I could have come here once with Papa,' she told herself regretfully.

Lord Seabrook wondered why she was looking unhappy and he longed to put his arms around her and comfort her, but then he told himself severely again that this was something he should not feel.

It was the reason he had hurried back to the castle and although his host and hostess had pressed him to stay longer at Inglewood, he could not suppress his eagerness to return.

They moved into another room and once again he asked himself how it was possible to feel like this for a woman he had only just met.

It was impossible for her to be of any consequence in his life, as he was very much aware of his position as head of the Brook family.

There were a great number of Brooks scattered through every part of England and Scotland and they all looked to him to uphold their name and to set an example to them all.

How, knowing that, could he do anything but marry someone whose lineage was as ancient and aristocratic as his own? Someone who would give him the son who would take his place in the castle when he died?

They wandered on from room to room.

As they ended up in the Picture Gallery, Lord Seabrook found himself puzzled by Lolita's intense interest and the emotions he could see clearly in her eyes and face.

'Why should any woman,' he mused, 'be so deeply moved by this undoubtedly beautiful and interesting building, but which is of no particular consequence to her?'

They walked downstairs to where at the back of the building was the Chapel which had been built by the monks. It was extremely beautiful and the stained glass windows would have been impressive even in a Cathedral.

The altar was of white marble and on it stood a jewelled cross which had been placed there when the Chapel was first completed.

Lolita felt as if her father had been with her ever since she had entered the Priory.

Now as they moved into the Chapel, she was vividly aware of her mother, almost as if she could see her.

She could feel her arms reaching out towards her and she could see the love in her eyes, which had always been there before she had been taken ill.

She forgot for a moment that she was with Lord Seabrook and Simon and without thinking she knelt down in the first pew facing the altar.

She clasped her hands together and closed her eyes.

She sensed that her mother was speaking to her and telling her how much she loved her and how both she and her father were looking after her. It was something Lolita had wanted to believe ever since she had run away.

Now it was as if her parents were speaking to her and reassuring her that she must never doubt again.

Lord Seabrook and Simon had just stood looking at her as she knelt down and now her eyes were closed in prayer.

Almost as if she had told Simon what to do he moved forward and knelt beside her.

Watching them Lord Seabrook drew in his breath. It was a long time since he had seen a woman praying so fervently.

He knew that for the moment everything was forgotten including Simon and himself.

It was at that instant that he admitted to himself that he could not bear to lose Mrs. Bell, whoever she might be.

Somehow he must contrive to keep her at the castle, whatever else she might want to do.

When they drove home Lolita was very silent.

But Simon was talking again. He was more interested in his pony, his dog and his swimming than in the big house they had just left.

"I will come swimming with you tomorrow morning," Lord Seabrook promised him. "Now I suggest, as I have some letters to write, that you ask Mrs. Bell to tell you more about the medieval monks who lived in the Priory."

"I want first to take Bracken for a walk," said Simon. "I know he's been very good while I have been away, but he will have missed me."

"Of course he has, so take him for a run in the garden before you go upstairs."

He was talking to Simon, but he kept looking at Lolita.

He still found it strange that she had been so overcome by the pictures and by the Priory itself.

Was it possible, he wondered, that her father had been an artist or perhaps her mother had been very religious.

The questions he wanted to ask her were tantalising him and yet he knew instinctively it would be a mistake for him to show too much curiosity.

Tea was waiting for them as soon as Simon had taken Bracken for a run over the lawns.

On Lord Seabrook's instructions Lolita poured out the tea.

"You are very silent," he said to her.

Simon had moved across the room with a plate on which he had crumbled a few biscuits for Bracken and he fed him on the bare boards by the window so that the dog did not make a mess on the carpet.

"I was thinking," said Lolita in reply to Lord Seabrook.

"That is obvious, but I am curious to know what is in your mind."

She paused for a moment.

"Actually I was wondering why you do not buy the Priory, my Lord. Your estate borders it and Simon will need somewhere to live one day when he marries."

Lord Seabrook stared at her in astonishment.

"I never thought of that and of course you are quite right. The Priory estate does indeed border with mine, although it is not so large. There is no reason why I should not farm more acres than I do already."

"It would be a great pity for anything so beautiful to pass into the hands of someone who would not really appreciate it," added Lolita. "And the pictures are so superb."

"I agree with you and I will certainly think about your idea. As I understand it the present owner is having difficulty in selling the Priory, so I should be able to obtain it at a reasonable price."

He rose from the table as he spoke and walked to the window.

He was not only thinking about the Priory, but how Lolita was unlike any other woman he had ever known.

If he had taken Catherine Cressington or any other London beauty round the Priory, they would have spoken effusively about the pictures and yet they would have made it very clear that they wanted them or others like them, as a present for themselves.

It seemed to him extraordinary that anyone so lovely as Lolita should have thought of Simon rather than herself and he was still mystified as to why she had been so moved by the Priory, especially when they were in the Chapel.

*

Lolita put Simon to bed and when she had wished him goodnight, she could not help wondering if Lord Seabrook, now they were alone in the castle, would ask her to join him for dinner.

There were no reasons why he should do so, but it would in fact be incorrect, as she was only a governess.

At the same time she thought he might feel lonely without someone to talk to.

She was quite right and when she walked into her own bedroom half-an-hour before it was time for dinner, there was a knock on the door.

When she opened it Lolita found Barty outside.

"His Lordship's compliments, Mrs. Bell, and he asks if you'll dine with him tonight as he wishes to discuss the future of Walcott Priory with you."

Lolita felt her heart turn a somersault.

"Tell his Lordship," she said in a controlled voice, "that I shall be delighted to join him for dinner."

When she closed the door she ran to the wardrobe to look at what was hanging there.

She wished she had some of the pretty gowns she had worn to parties in London, as she had brought only the lightest and plainest of her dresses as she had no wish to look conspicuous wherever she went.

The gown she chose was white as was correct for a *debutante* and clung to her figure.

When she walked into the study to find Lord Seabrook waiting for her, he thought she looked even more like a Goddess from Olympus than ever before.

Because he had only given her a little time to make herself ready, Lolita had merely brushed her hair until it was neat and tidy.

The only jewels she wore were a single row of small pearls and her mother's ring was still on her finger. She was careful not to show the palm of her hand as if anyone could see the diamonds they would know it was not a wedding ring.

Lord Seabrook in his evening clothes looked even more distinguished than in the daytime.

As Lolita walked towards him she thought that, if he was escorting her to the smartest ball ever given in London, she would be proud that he was her partner.

Lord Seabrook was thinking exactly the same.

There was no beauty, including Lady Cressington, who could compare with the loveliness of Lolita.

'She shines because her beauty is natural and uncontrived,' he thought. 'She is like a lily in a garden or a star in the sky above.'

Barty announced that dinner was served and Lord Seabrook escorted Lolita into the dining room.

Because he did not want to talk about buying the Priory in front of the servants, they discussed its contents, most especially the pictures.

"I cannot understand," said Lord Seabrook, "how the Earl of Walcott could have parted with his possessions, which were so intimate that they should have been preserved for his children, even if he could not keep the Priory itself."

"I am sure that was what the Earl wanted," responded Lolita. "But perhaps fate or rather his poverty was against him. As you must be aware, my Lord, those pictures are today very valuable."

"I have always understood that the Earl died without having a son, but I would have thought some relation would have come forward and demanded to be allowed to keep just a few of the treasures in the family."

He spoke almost harshly – it was as if he was accusing him of giving up his heritage without even fighting to preserve it.

"I am sure that was what the Earl wanted to happen, but of course he would not have sold the Priory in the first place if he had not been forced to do so."

She spoke a little truculently and Lord Seabrook smiled.

"I see you are defending him," he said, "but at the time by hook or by crook he should have kept some of the pictures at any rate. I noticed that there was one of his daughter when she was very small and even that one was left behind."

Lolita did not answer and because he had not wished to argue the point, Lord Seabrook changed the subject.

When dinner was over they walked into the drawing room where the chandeliers had been lit.

"Now I can talk to you about whether or not I should buy the Priory," sighed Lord Seabrook as he sank into a comfortable armchair.

"I have already suggested that you might give it to Simon when he marries, my Lord, but of course by that time you may have a son of your own who will want somewhere to live if you are still alive."

"Which I hope I shall be, but the difficulty is that to have a son, I have first to be married."

To his surprise Lolita rose to her feet.

"You must forgive me," she said, "but I must go to bed. I am very tired and I want to feel at my best when you swim with Simon and me tomorrow morning."

Lord Seabrook also rose.

"Of course I understand. It has been a long day. Good night, Mrs. Bell, and thank you once again for helping me to enjoy my dinner."

Lolita smiled at him and then without saying any more and before he could reach the door she had left the room.

135

Lord Seabrook walked to the window.

The last rays of the sun were crimson on the horizon and the stars were coming out overhead and were reflected in the stillness of the lake below.

It was very beautiful and very romantic.

Suddenly he knew he could not go on any longer.

He wanted Mrs. Bell unbearably.

He could no longer pretend, as he had tried to do, that she meant nothing to him and was just a competent governess for his nephew.

He stood looking at the lake for a long time before he turned and walked from the room and upstairs.

Lolita had torn herself away from him – not because she was tired, but because she had an almost irresistible urge to tell him who she was and to explain why she had been so emotional at seeing the Priory.

How could she bear to allow all those treasures which were so precious to her mother and father to fall into the hands of someone unknown and uninterested, perhaps a common man who was only buying it all because he was rich enough to afford it.

'They are mine! They are part of me!' Lolita anguished. 'I cannot bear them to belong to someone who will not love and cherish them as I could do.'

As she climbed into bed she knew it would be impossible to sleep.

All she wanted to do was to talk to her parents and to ask them to explain to her why she had felt so moved at Walcott Priory and what it had meant to them in their lives.

It had never seemed quite so important as it did now as when they had talked about it, it did not seem real.

Now she had seen it, she had felt the atmosphere which seemed vibrant with the Walcotts all down the centuries.

There were several books beside her bed with she had taken from the library, but she thought it would be almost impossible to concentrate on reading at the moment.

She therefore picked up her Prayer Book which she had brought with her when she had run away. She thought that if she prayed as she had done in the Chapel, she would feel once again as if her father and mother were beside her.

They would tell her what she should do.

Then to her surprise the door which led into the schoolroom opened.

It was ajar in case Simon should call for her in the night and she thought it must be Simon coming in, but to her surprise it was his uncle.

He closed the door behind him and walked down the room towards her.

"What has – happened? What is – wrong?" stammered Lolita. "I didn't hear – Simon call for me."

"Simon is fast asleep," Lord Seabrook assured her. "But I want to talk to you."

"To talk – to me!" exclaimed Lolita. "But what about – and why here?"

"You left me before I had a chance to tell you what was in my mind," he replied. "I have thought about it for several nights and I have no wish to go on thinking about it again tonight."

He had reached the bed and now he sat down on it. "I do not understand," murmured Lolita.

"It is really quite simple," said Lord Seabrook with a smile. "I think, although you are very mysterious about it, that you are as lonely as I am. If we share our loneliness then perhaps we can make each other very happy, as I certainly want to make *you* happy."

He spoke very quietly, but Lolita's eyes were still wide with surprise.

She still did not understand.

"You are very lovely," he added. "So lovely that it would be impossible for any man not to want to make you happy. I think we can find a great deal of happiness and joy together."

There was a moment's silence and then as Lolita was still staring at him, he continued,

"I will promise you one thing. You will never again have to earn your own living or be frightened. I will protect and look after you and I will be very generous if in the future we agree to part from each other."

As he finished speaking, he moved forward as if to put his arms round her.

Lolita pushed herself backwards against the pillows.

"I still do not understand," she said. "What are you saying to me and what do you want?"

"The answer to that question is quite simple. I want you, my darling. I want you in my arms and I want to teach you about love, the love I have been feeling for you for a long time."

"It cannot – be true," whispered Lolita.

"It *is* true," he answered, "and as I have already said, I feel sure we will be very happy together."

He moved a little closer still, but she held herself away from him and when his lips would have found hers, she turned her head away.

"What are you – asking me to do?" she asked.

Then as if it suddenly occurred to her, she gave a little cry.

"You cannot be suggesting – that I should be your – *mistress.*"

"That is rather a hard word. I love you, Lolo, but I cannot, in my position, ask you to be my wife. Because you are so intelligent I feel you will understand the situation. I will give you anything you want and everything you ask of me."

Lolita gave a little cry of horror.

"N-no! N-no!" she stuttered. "Of course *not!*"

"I will not allow you to say that!"

His arms were round her and he pulled her closer.

She managed somehow to twist round so that her hands were holding him away from her.

"No! No!" she repeated. "No, I could not – do such – a thing. Go away. Please go away – I must not listen – to you."

There was such agony in her voice that Lord Seabrook checked himself.

"Please believe," he said soothingly, "that I love you as I have never loved any woman before. You must understand why I cannot marry you, but I know I can make you happy, as I shall be happy just because we are together."

"It would be – wrong – wicked, and it is – something I cannot do. It would shock and – horrify Mama."

The words seemed to force themselves through Lolita's lips and although she was almost incoherent, Lord Seabrook could only just hear her.

For a moment he was silent and then he moved a little away from her hands which were still outstretched on his chest.

As he did so he saw the light of the candle glitter on the third finger of her left hand.

He was aware it was her wedding ring.

Then she moved her hand as if she realised there was no longer any need to hold him away from her.

"So you are not married. I suspected it, but there was really no reason to disbelieve you."

"I thought it would make me seem – older – when I was bringing Simon to you," muttered Lolita.

"So you are not married," Lord Seabrook repeated as if he was speaking to himself. "That makes matters rather different from what I had thought and what I calculated we might feel for each other."

Lolita turned to look at him and he saw there were tears in her eyes.

"Go away! Please go away! You are – frightening me and there is no one to help me now that – Papa and Mama are dead."

Lord Seabrook rose to his feet.

"Forgive me," he said. "The last thing I wanted was to upset you. Just go to sleep and forget what I have just suggested."

He looked down at her thinking that it was impossible for anyone to look so lovely and yet so helpless.

"It has been a complete misunderstanding on my part," he added quietly. Please forgive me and try to forget it has ever happened."

Lolita did not answer him and after a moment he turned and walked back towards the door.

He went into the schoolroom and she heard the outer door into the passage close very quietly.

It was then she knew he had left her and felt the tears running down her cheeks.

'I love him. *I love him*. But how can I do anything which would shock Mama and Papa if they knew about it?'

She turned round and hid her face in the pillows.

Then almost as if she was being directed by a voice within herself, she climbed out of bed and walked to the cupboard where her case had been put after it had been unpacked by one of the housemaids.

She brought it out and placed it on one of the chairs and then slowly, as if it was an effort, she dressed herself in the clothes she had arrived in – the blue dress and jacket which she had felt was so unobtrusive when she left her stepfather's house.

She took down her other gowns from the wardrobe and packed them into the case, together with the one she had worn for dinner. It took her a little time to add her brush and comb and her shoes.

At last she was ready and tiptoed to the door which led into the corridor.

She peeped out.

The Master Suite was on the lower floor and no one else would be awake at this hour.

Carrying her case in one hand and her handbag which contained her money in the other, she moved quietly into the corridor.

She considered it would not be safe to go down the side staircase as one of the servants might see her, so instead she walked down to the first floor and to the top of the main staircase.

There were only a few lights burning in the sconces and there was no night-footman on duty in the castle as her stepfather had insisted on having in London.

Silently Lolita walked down the stairs and reached the front door which was not bolted.

As she pulled the door open she found herself face to face with Lord Seabrook.

He was as surprised to see her as she was to see him and for a moment they both stared at each other.

Then in a strange voice which did not sound like his own he asked,

"Where are you going?"

"A-away," Lolita stammered. "I-I have to go away."

"Why?"

"B-because I am f-frightened."

Her words were hardly audible.

"Of me?"

Now she was looking into his eyes and without thinking she told him the truth.

"N-no, but I am frightened of – doing what you have asked me to do."

For a moment neither of them moved and Lord Seabrook said,

"I swear to you on everything that is Holy I will never ask you to do that again."

He saw as he spoke Lolita's expression change and there was a sudden light in her eyes almost as if it was reflected from the stars.

"You are quite safe here," he continued quietly. "Go back to bed, Lolo, and forget what has happened. It was very wrong of me and I can only apologise to you."

She did not answer and he was aware that she gave a little sigh as if of relief.

"Go to bed," he told her again gently. "We will talk about it all tomorrow. Just forgive me for being very stupid and think of Simon."

She looked at him as if she had not heard correctly what he was saying.

Next he took her case from her and as he did so she turned and ran up the stairs very swiftly without looking back.

By the time he reached the first landing he was aware that she had gone up the other staircase and he heard her bedroom door close.

He carried her case up the stairs and when he reached the top he opened the door of her bedroom and placed it inside.

He closed the door again and walked slowly back the way he had come.

He had no idea that Lolita was standing just inside the door listening to his footsteps fading away.

She was wondering frantically if she should go after him.

CHAPTER SEVEN

Lolita was asleep when the maid called her.

After she had drawn back the curtains, the maid came towards the bed just as Lolita opened her eyes.

"It's nearly eight o'clock, ma'am, but there's no need to hurry. His Lordship's said he'd like you and Master Simon to come to the stables at half-past-eight."

Lolita was surprised, but she did not say anything to the maid. Instead she walked through the schoolroom into Simon's room to see if he was awake.

He was sitting up in bed playing with some toy soldiers he had found in the fort which had once been his father's.

"Your uncle wants you to ride with him at half-past eight," Lolita told him.

"Yes, I know and I'm going to show him how I can ride so that he'll give me a bigger horse, though I still love my pony."

"I think you would be wise to stay with your pony, because he is beginning to do exactly what you want him to do and I think he loves you too."

Simon considered this for a moment with his head on one side.

"Do you think my pony loves me as much as Bracken does?"

"I'm sure of it, and remember it's always wise to stay with the animals and people you love."

As if she could not help herself she bent down and kissed Simon, who did not seem surprised and put his arms round her neck.

"I love you, Lolo," he said.

"And I love you too, Simon."

She returned to her room.

She could not imagine how last night she had been thinking only of Lord Seabrook and not of Simon when she had started to run away and she realised now that she would have been desperately ashamed of herself for deserting him.

But at the same time she loved Lord Seabrook and it would be extremely difficult to be with him every day without his becoming aware that she loved him.

'He must never know,' she thought.

She remembered how he had turned away from Lady Cressington in disgust.

'I could not bear him to feel like that about me,' she told herself as she dressed.

When she and Simon reached the stables they found Lord Seabrook waiting for them.

Lolita could not help her heart turning several somersaults, nor could she prevent the light shining in her eyes that had not been there before.

His Lordship had chosen a new horse for her and it was very spirited and hard to handle, while he himself was mounted on a new stallion which he had bought from the same breeder who had sold him Simon's pony.

They were both having difficulty with their horses and Lolita realised that it was his way of coping with an uncomfortable moment after the drama of last night.

'He is so clever,' she told herself, 'and very, very intelligent.'

As soon as possible they gave their horses their heads and after a good run they both calmed down a little.

When they reached the end of a long gallop, Lord Seabrook, having arrived first, watched Lolita join him.

The words he wanted to say to her trembled on his lips, but he told himself it was too soon and certainly not the right moment.

"I think we should return to the castle," he suggested. "You and Simon will be feeling hungry, having to wait so long for your breakfast."

Simon caught up with them at that moment. He had been riding very well and had gone faster than ever.

"I think, my Lord," she said, "if we give Simon a start he would really be able to race us and it would mean a great deal to him."

"And, I think, to you. Am I to let him win?"

"No, of course not," replied Lolita. "But if it was a close finish it would make him even more enthusiastic than he is now."

"That is just what we will do."

Lord Seabrook told Simon the plan of the race and then he sent the groom ahead to wait at what he decided would be the winning post and be ready to declare the winner.

The groom smiled and set off.

Lord Seabrook gave Simon a very good start and a smaller one for Lolita.

"If I beat you," she said encouragingly, "it will be a miracle."

"You would hardly want me to give you the race."

"No certainly not, but I think you are overestimating my skill."

"That would be impossible!"

He rode away as he spoke and she wondered exactly what he meant. But it was very exciting to be with him and riding such an outstanding horse.

'How could I have been so stupid as to want to run away?' she asked herself again and again.

Then she was worrying that Lord Seabrook might guess how happy she was to stay at the castle and be so close to him.

The race was a great success. Lord Seabrook with a superb exhibition of riding managed to arrange that he won by only half a length from Simon with Lolita a respectable third.

She pulled in her horse when she realised what Lord Seabrook was planning to do and she found Simon's excitement at such a close finish was very lovable.

She wanted to hug him and Lord Seabrook too, but she told herself that was the sort of thing she must not think about.

They rode slowly back to the castle and when they had handed their horses over to the grooms, Simon called,

"I'm very hungry."

"And I am too," said Lord Seabrook. "So we will just go straight into the breakfast room and change our boots and everything else afterwards."

Lolita just took off her riding jacket and her hat.

Barty had a large breakfast waiting for them and Simon enjoyed every mouthful.

When they had finished Lord Seabrook said,

"I expect as it is a lovely warm day you will be going down to the lake to swim. I will come and join you, but I have some letters to sign first."

"I want to race you in the lake as well," challenged Simon. "But I expect you will be too fast for me."

"I would hope so, but it is a long time since I swam and I may have forgotten how to. So if I sink, you will have to rescue me."

"I think Lolo would save you."

"And if she could not manage it, I would drown, and what would you do then?"

Simon put his hand into his uncle's.

"I love you, Uncle James, and I love being here at the castle with Bracken and my pony. You must promise me to be very careful, because if you drowned or died like Papa, Lolo and I would have nowhere to go."

"You are quite right," answered Lord Seabrook, visibly touched by Simon's words, "and I promise you I will be very careful of myself and of you."

They were talking as they left the breakfast room and climbed upstairs.

Lord Seabrook left Lolita at the first floor and walked towards the Master Suite.

The maid was waiting in the schoolroom to take off Simon's riding boots and Lolita went on to her own room, wondering as she took off her riding clothes,

'Would it be embarrassing to swim in my bathing suit in front of Lord Seabrook? Perhaps it would be wiser if I watched him and Simon from the shore.'

It only took her a second or two to make up her mind and firmly she put on one of the light dresses she had brought with her.

She was just tying the band round her waist when she heard a carriage draw up on the gravel outside as the windows of the schoolroom and her bedroom overlooked the front of the house.

Hoping it was not a visitor who would delay Lord Seabrook, she ran to the window and looked out.

There was a carriage below which she knew was a post-chaise and it was drawn by two horses which meant it had travelled some distance.

She wondered who it could be.

And then with a feeling of horror she recognised the head and shoulders of the man who was alighting.

It was her stepfather.

She gave a sudden cry.

Then running across the bedroom she opened the door and ran down the stairs to the first landing.

It flashed through Lolita's mind that Lord Seabrook might be changed by now and have gone down to his study.

But as she rushed along the passage to the Master Suite, she saw his valet coming out of the room carrying his Lordship's riding boots and breeches.

She swept past the valet who looked at her in surprise and, pulling open the door without knocking, she burst into Lord Seabrook's bedroom.

He was standing in front of his dressing table putting the finishing touches to the tie he had just fastened round his neck.

As Lolita ran towards him he stared at her in astonishment.

Without pausing she flung herself against him.

"Hide me! Hide me!" she pleaded almost incoherently. "Take me where *he* cannot find me."

Lord Seabrook's arms went straight round her.

"What is the matter?" he implored her. "What has upset you?"

"It's my – stepfather," Lolita gasped. "He has found out – where I am and has come – to take me away. Oh,*please*, please hide me!"

Lord Seabrook held her a little closer.

"No one shall take you away if you do not wish to go," he said stoutly.

"But he can," screamed Lolita frantically. "He is my – Guardian and by law I have to do – what he tells me."

"And what does he want you to do?"

"He wants – me to marry a – ghastly awful man – because he is rich – and important."

He could hardly hear her words as they tumbled out.

As if the agony of telling him was too much for her,

Lolita hid her face against his shoulder.

"So this is why you ran away," said Lord Seabrook quietly, "and it was a very sensible action for you to take. Now tell me what is your name and the name of your stepfather?"

Lolita paused and with an effort, she managed to say,

"I am – Lolita Vernon and my father – was the last – Earl of Walcott."

Lord Seabrook gave a gasp.

"Why on earth didn't you tell me?"

"Because I knew my stepfather would search for me and – take me back."

"I told you I will not allow him to do so."

"How can you – stop him?"

Lolita raised her head and looked up at him and he could see the terror in her eyes and feel the fear which made her tremble in his arms.

"Do you really think, my lovely one," he asked softly,

"I could possibly lose you now? You need not be afraid. I promise you that your stepfather will not take you away."

He realised that Lolita was trying to believe what he was saying.

Lord Seabrook released her from his tight hold.

"I will go downstairs," he said, "and talk to your stepfather and you shall hear every word I say to him."

"*I cannot see him*," cried Lolita. "Just tell him – I am not here – I have left and you have – no idea where I am."

"And where would you go?" he enquired, "where you would not be afraid he would follow you and find you? And how could you possibly leave Simon and me alone?"

Lolita looked at him, but she did not answer.

He smiled at her tenderly.

"You will have to trust me and I promise you that your stepfather will leave without you and that you will stay here with me."

"How can you be sure? He is very powerful – because he is so rich."

"I suppose that is why your mother married him."

"Of course it was. She loved Papa and no one could ever take his place in her life. But she was so worried about me because we were so very, very poor and so she married him – although he was not in any way like Papa."

"I know now," he said, "why you prayed to your mother yesterday in the Chapel at the Priory. I think you should trust her and me to prevent you from having to do anything which would make you unhappy and miserable."

"I want to believe you, but be very careful of Stepfather. He is very powerful as I have already told you and he has the law on his side."

Even as she finished speaking there was a knock on the door. Lord Seabrook moved a little further away from her. "Come in."

It was Barty who entered the bedroom.

"Excuse me, my Lord," he said, "but there's a gentleman called Mr. Piran who wishes to see you on what he says is a most important matter."

"I am just coming down, Barty. Offer him some refreshment and I presume you have put him in my study."

"Yes, my Lord."

Barty left the room closing the door behind him.

Lord Seabrook reached out his hands to Lolita.

"I have asked you to trust me and I promise you again faithfully that whatever your stepfather says or does you will remain here at the castle with me and Simon."

He took Lolita's hands in his as he finished speaking. They were very cold and her fingers were trembling.

"You have been very brave and very clever," he told her quietly, "and you will have to go on being brave and clever for a little while longer yet. Then it will all be over and you can be yourself as I have always wanted you to be."

Lolita drew in her breath.

"How can you be – *so sure*?" she asked him with pleading eyes.

"That is what you are going to overhear."

"I – cannot – meet – him," whispered Lolita.

"I said you are going to hear what I am going to say and I will show you how it will be done."

He drew her out of the room along the passage and down the stairs.

They walked towards the study and Lolita was just about to protest again that she could not meet her stepfather when Lord Seabrook stopped and opened a door.

It was, Lolita knew, the door to the tapestry room.

They had not used it since she had been at the castle.

It was quite an attractive room, the walls hung with ancient tapestries instead of pictures, which gave the room a rather doleful atmosphere.

There was a fireplace at one end of the room and on either side of it were bookcases.

Lord Seabrook took her to the one to the left of the fireplace and to her surprise when they reached it, he touched something on one side and the two top rows swung open.

She realised that there was a small opening in the side nearest the fireplace and through it she could look right into the study.

It was an ancient listening place, which must have been made hundreds of years earlier and this, she thought, had helped to ensure the safety of whoever was in charge of the castle in those times.

It meant that the Chieftain was always under the surveillance of his bodyguard, even when anyone he was interviewing believed they were alone with him.

Before opening the bookcase Lord Seabrook had put his finger to his lips as he moved away from Lolita.

Walking as lightly as he could on the carpet so that he would not be heard, he closed the door behind him without making a sound and Lolita could hear his footsteps in the passage leading to the door of the study.

She held her breath as she heard the door open and she put her eye to the watch-hole.

She could see her stepfather quite clearly as he rose from the chair where he had been sitting in front of the fireplace.

He was looking just as she had remembered – somewhat overwhelming and pleased with himself.

Yet when Lord Seabrook joined him, Ralph Piran suddenly seemed to look somewhat inferior.

The bluster so characteristic of his personality was an unpleasant contrast to the quiet politeness of Lord Seabrook.

"You have asked to see me, Mr. Piran," he began as he reached him and held out his hand.

"I will come straight to the point, Lord Seabrook. I have come here because I understand you have in your household a young woman who calls herself Mrs. Bell and who is acting as governess to your nephew."

"I should be interested to know who gave you this particular information."

"I was having luncheon in White's Club three days ago with Lord Stapleford, who is on the Board of one of my companies. He was greeted by a young man called Captain Michael Duncan, who I learned had recently been staying with you."

"That is true."

"He informed Lord Stapleford that the jewellery which had been stolen from his father had now been recovered and it had been found in your castle."

Lord Seabrook nodded but did not reply.

Listening Lolita thought no one watching him would think he was wondering why this information should concern him in any way.

"When Lord Stapleford asked how you were," Ralph Piran continued, "Captain Duncan replied that you were in excellent form and had employed, in his opinion, the most beautiful governess for your nephew he had ever seen in his whole life!"

His voice sharpened as he went on,

"In fact he described her so accurately that I recognised the 'Mrs. Bell' he was talking about as my stepdaughter, who had run away from me in an extremely annoying fashion just a short time ago."

"Your stepdaughter!" exclaimed Lord Seabrook. "But why should she have run away?"

"For no sensible reason. But as you will not know, her name is not Mrs. Bell but Lady Lolita Vernon. As her legal Guardian, now that her father is dead, I am here to take her back with me."

There was a pause before Lord Seabrook declared,

"I am afraid that is impossible."

"What do you mean *impossible*?" Ralph Piran demanded in a very different tone of voice. "I need my stepdaughter with me and she must return to London to take her place in the Social world in which she has just made her debut."

"I think, as she has just recently learnt of her mother's death," said Lord Seabrook quietly, "that is something she will have no wish to do. In fact she does not wish to go to London at all, but to stay here in Ullswater."

"If that is your attitude, my Lord," snarled Ralph Piran angrily, "it is something I am prepared to fight. When I leave here I shall go straight to see the Senior Police Officer of the district and demand his assistance in making my position as my stepdaughter's Guardian crystal clear to you."

"I am afraid whatever steps you may take," Lord Seabrook told him, "they will be too late."

"What do you mean by that?" demanded Ralph Piran. "How could what I demand possibly be too late? The law, as your Lordship well knows, is the law."

"I am well aware of the law of the land, but I think the Senior Police Officer, who of course I know well, will be reluctant to bring into action any aspect of the law against my wife."

There was a sudden silence while Ralph Piran stared at Lord Seabrook.

Then as Lolita held her breath, he managed to blurt out, "Did you say your – *wife*?"

"We are actually," replied Lord Seabrook calmly, "being married tonight by the Bishop of Carlisle who is incidentally a relative of mine. I think, Mr. Piran, if you attempted to prevent the ceremony taking place, you would become the victim of the Press who would make a laughingstock of you."

Again there was a silence.

"You really intend to marry my stepdaughter?"

"We love each other," said Lord Seabrook, "and I know we will be very happy. As it would obviously upset Lolita to have to meet you and to be forced to listen to any reproaches or criticism of her behaviour, I can only ask you to leave my castle quietly and at once without seeing her."

He waited for Ralph Piran to respond and as he did not do so he continued,

"Perhaps, after we have had our honeymoon and settled down, I will bring Lolita to London, and if you wish to meet her at my house in Grosvenor Square, I am sure she would wish to hear about her mother's funeral from you and to collect any personal belongings she may have left behind."

Ralph Piran was defeated.

He was too intelligent not to realise the obvious and with an obvious effort he managed to mutter,

"There is nothing I can say, my Lord, except that I hope Lolita will be very happy with you. As you have suggested, we could meet when you visit London."

He made a gesture with his hands.

"I would of course like to be present at your wedding,but as that might prove embarrassing I will keep all I have to tell her until we meet."

"Thank you, Mr. Piran, for understanding the situation and accepting it, as I thought you would, in a manner which will make Lolita very happy."

He spoke in a more friendly tone as he added,

"She has, I know, no wish to quarrel with anyone, but I can only comment on her courage in running away, and it was most fortunate I was able to offer her the security of my castle."

"Of course, of course," Ralph Piran agreed. "And now, as there is nothing more which need concern us, I will return to Penrith, where I can easily catch a train to London."

"That is indeed true, and it would be extremely kind of you, Mr. Piran, if you would send here as soon as possible all Lolita's clothes which she left behind in London."

The two men were moving towards the door as he spoke.

Just for a moment Ralph Piran hesitated.

It was as if he thought he was being made use of, which was something he resented.

Then because he had always been impressed by titles and those who held them, he managed to reply quite pleasantly,

"Of course I will do so, my Lord. The trunks shall be brought to you by one of my staff so there will be no chance of their being stolen on the journey."

"That is most kind of you and I am indeed grateful."

They walked out of the study and Lolita heard them moving down the passage towards the hall.

As they passed the door of the tapestry room she stood very still and listened intently until she could no longer hear any footsteps.

Her stepfather was leaving and when he was gone she would be safe.

He could no longer hurt her and no longer drag her back to London to make her accept the advances and the touch of the repulsive Murdock Tanner.

She was free and she could be herself again at last.

She was her father and mother's daughter and need no longer be afraid.

The door of the tapestry room opened and Lord Seabrook entered, closing the door behind him and standing still.

He was looking at Lolita as if he had never seen her before. As their eyes met he held out his arms.

Without thinking of anything except that he had saved her, she ran towards him and flung herself against him just as she had when she had run into his bedroom.

"Thank you – thank you," she tried to say.

But his arms tightened round her and his lips came down on hers.

He kissed her and Lolita knew that this was exactly how she believed a kiss would be – only it was a million times more wonderful.

Lord Seabrook kissed her and carried on kissing her until her body melted into his.

Lolita felt she was no longer herself but a part of him.

Their love enveloped both of them like the sunshine.

Lord Seabrook raised his head.

"*I love you!* God, how I love you! How could you have been so skilful in deceiving us for so long by pretending to be a governess?"

"You know now – why I was so frightened," Lolita managed to say. "My stepfather would, I know, have forced me to marry – that horrible, beastly man whom he respects so much, because – he is so rich."

She was speaking once again in a frightened voice and Lord Seabrook kissed her into silence.

Only when her body was quivering against his, not from fear but from the wild emotions he evoked in her did he tell her,

"Forget everything except that we are to be married tonight and then you will be mine."

"Are you really marrying me?" asked Lolita excitedly. "How could you decide to do so when you did not know who I was?"

"I knew when you tried to run away last night," he said, "that I could not lose you. If you had committed a dozen murders or your father had done so, I would still want you as my wife."

Lolita put out her hand to gently touch his cheek.

"That was very brave of you and I thought that although I loved you – you would never love me because I was only a governess."

"A very unusual and a very beautiful governess!" he exclaimed, looking deeply into her eyes. "But as it is impossible for me to live without you, nothing matters except that you should be mine."

He held her a little closer.

"Now I can understand what you were feeling yesterday in the Priory."

Lolita put back her head and looked up at him.

"When I prayed in the Chapel, I felt that both Mama and Papa were telling me that everything would be all right – and that I need no longer be frightened. And now it has all come true."

"Do you love me?" he asked her tenderly.

"I love you with all my heart and soul," Lolita whispered. "But I was so afraid that you would find out and send me away in disgust."

He gave a little laugh.

"I have loved you from the first moment I saw you. I tried to fight against it, but our love, my precious, was too strong for both of us. That is why I am not going to wait a moment longer than I need. I actually wrote to the Bishop and sent the letter early this morning before breakfast. Because he has always been fond of me, I know he will do as I ask."

He pulled her a little closer.

"Tell me again that you love me and you want to be my wife."

"I love you with every fibre of my being, and I can imagine nothing more wonderful in the whole world – than being married to you."

She put her arms round his neck.

"Can I really stay here in this fabulous, adorable castle with you for ever?"

"That is just what I want," he said, "and of course we must have children, my darling, to play with Simon and they must never be lonely or ill-treated as he has been."

"I would never have dreamed that I would ever be – the mother of – your sons."

Because he was moved by her words, Lord Seabrook kissed her again.

Now his kisses were becoming more possessive and passionate.

Lolita felt as if a growing flicker of fire was moving through her body and into her breast.

She knew now this was what she had felt the very first moment she had met Lord Seabrook, but it had not been so exciting or intense as it was now.

"I love you – I adore you," she repeated over and over again.

Because he could find no words to express his deepest feelings, Lord Seabrook merely kissed her again.

They both felt they were flying up into the sky. It was with an effort that he moved her to one side.

"Now we must be sensible, my darling, because I want to tell you what plans I have made. Also we have to ask Mrs. Shepherd to provide you with the wedding gown and veil which all the Seabrook brides have worn in the past."

"It is difficult to think of anything – but you," murmured Lolita.

"If you look at me like that I shall kiss you forever," he smiled, "and then you will never hear my plans."

She slipped her hand into his.

"Sit down and tell me what they are."

There was a sofa just behind them and they sat down as if they were both a little weak at the knees.

"What I had planned," Lord Seabrook began, "is that the Bishop should marry us here in my own Chapel, which is very ancient, as you know, but not quite as beautiful as the one at the Priory."

As if she knew what he was going to say next, Lolita looked at him wide-eyed.

"I am now going to arrange that we are married at the Priory and I think we should stay there for the first few nights of our honeymoon."

"That would be so wonderful and I am so very happy."

"As I will always be and, my darling, I have already arranged that while we are on our honeymoon, which can be either at the Priory or here, Simon will go for a trip on the yacht with the Captain. Mrs. Shepherd will go with them to look after him and I have learned that the Captain has two sons, one of them the same age as Simon and one a year older."

He saw the delight come in Lolita's eyes.

"I think the boy will enjoy himself and not miss us too much. Later you and I will use the yacht to go abroad, where I will buy you the trousseau which you should have before your wedding, but which you will have afterwards and which will make you look even more beautiful than you do already."

Lolita gave a cry.

"It is the most wonderful perfect plan I have ever heard – and only you could have thought of it."

"Now," Lord Seabrook told her, "you will understand that I am going to be very busy making all the wedding arrangements, so you must break it gently to Simon what is happening. As I do not want him to feel he is being left out, I thought he could give you away."

Lolita gave another cry of delight.

"The only other people who will be present as witnesses when we are married will be Barty and Mrs. Shepherd, who have both looked after me for so many years."

"It is just the wedding I would really want!" exclaimed Lolita, "without all those silly women sniggering and saying how lucky I am to marry you and being jealous because they are not the bride."

She was thinking of Lady Cressington and Lord Seabrook felt he could read her thoughts.

"What you say is indeed true and I never wanted to marry anyone until I met you. There has always been something about them which I thought was wrong although I could not put a name to it. But I now know what it is."

"What is it?" asked Lolita.

"It is because, my darling, you are good, pure and innocent. It is something so special I have always wanted in my wife, but thought I would never find it, however hard I looked."

"I want to be all those things for you and I know it is what my mother always wanted me to be."

"It is what you are and you will be the same forever."

Then he was kissing her again wildly and passionately.

Yet at the same time there was a touch of reverence in his kisses.

She was so perfect and unblemished and exactly what he wanted his wife to be.

Once again they were flying up to the sky.

Lolita knew she had found the Love which is Divine.

The Love for which she had prayed and known in her heart that God would give to her.

It was the Love which would last all through their life together.

The Love which would carry them into Eternity and from which there is no end.

35465835R00098

Printed in Poland
by Amazon Fulfillment
Poland Sp. z o.o., Wrocław